Welcome to the world of Sydney Harbour Hospital

(or *SHH...* for short— because secrets never stay hidden for long!)

Looking out over cosmopolitan Sydney Harbour, Australia's premier teaching hospital is a hive of round-the-clock activity—with a *very* active hospital grapevine.

With the most renowned (and gorgeous!) doctors in Sydney working side by side, professional and sensual tensions run sky-high—there's *always* plenty of romantic rumours to gossip about...

Who's been kissing who in the on-call room? What's going on between legendary heart surgeon Finn Kennedy and tough-talking A&E doctor Evie Lockheart? And what's wrong with Finn?

Find out in this enthralling new eight-book continuity from Medical Romance™—indulge yourself with eight helpings of romance, emotion and gripping medical drama!

Sydney Harbour Hospital
From saving lives to sizzling seduction, these doctors are the very best!

Dear Reader

Preparing to write the last of the *Sydney Harbour Hospital* series was a bit daunting. I knew that there would be fantastic books behind me, and that there would be things that I had to wrap up, so it was with some trepidation that I finally sat down to write James and Ava's story.

And then I fell in love.

I know that sounds mushy, but I honestly fell in love with both my hero and heroine and, as painful as it was at times, it was a story that was an absolute pleasure to write.

Relationships fall apart, marriages fall apart and sometimes life is hard—James and Ava both had every reason to call it a day… Except I didn't want them to.

I hope that a few pages in you don't want them to either.

Happy reading!

Carol x

SYDNEY HARBOUR HOSPITAL: AVA'S RE-AWAKENING

BY
CAROL MARINELLI

For Anne Gracie. Thank you for your friendship and support. It means a lot. Carol x

First published in Great Britain 2012
by Mills & Boon, an imprint of Harlequin (UK) Limited.
Large Print edition 2013
Harlequin (UK) Limited, Eton House,
18-24 Paradise Road, Richmond, Surrey TW9 1SR

Special thanks and acknowledgement are given to Carol Marinelli for her contribution to the *Sydney Harbour Hospital* series.

ISBN: 978 0 263 23085 7

Harlequin (UK) policy is to use papers that are natural, renewable and recyclable products and made from wood grown in sustainable forests. The logging and manufacturing process conform to the legal environmental regulations of the country of origin.

Printed and bound in Great Britain
by CPI Antony Rowe, Chippenham, Wiltshire

Praise for
Carol Marinelli:

'A heartwarming story about taking a chance and not letting the past destroy the future. It is strengthened by two engaging lead characters and a satisfying ending.'
—*RT Book Reviews* on
THE LAST KOLOVSKY PLAYBOY

'Carol Marinelli writes with sensitivity, compassion and understanding, and RESCUING PREGNANT CINDERELLA is not just a powerful romance but an uplifting and inspirational tale about starting over, new beginnings and moving on.'
—*Cataromance* on
ST PIRAN'S: RESCUING PREGNANT CINDERELLA

If you love Carol Marinelli,
you'll fall head over heels for her
sparkling, touching, witty debut
PUTTING ALICE BACK TOGETHER—
available from MIRA Books

Sydney Harbour Hospital

Sexy surgeons, dedicated doctors,
scandalous secrets, on-call dramas...

Welcome to the world of Sydney Harbour Hospital (or *SHH...* for short— because secrets never stay hidden for long!)

New nurse Lily got caught up in the hotbed of hospital gossip in
SYDNEY HARBOUR HOSPITAL: LILY'S SCANDAL
by Marion Lennox

And gorgeous paediatrician Teo came to single mum Zoe's rescue in
SYDNEY HARBOUR HOSPITAL: ZOE'S BABY
by Alison Roberts

Then sexy Sicilian playboy Luca finally met his match in
SYDNEY HARBOUR HOSPITAL: LUCA'S BAD GIRL
by Amy Andrews

And Hayley opened Tom's eyes to love in
SYDNEY HARBOUR HOSPITAL: TOM'S REDEMPTION
by Fiona Lowe

Heiress Lexi learned to put the past behind her in
SYDNEY HARBOUR HOSPITAL: LEXI'S SECRET
by Melanie Milburne

And adventurer Charlie helped shy Bella fulfil her dreams— and find love on the way!
SYDNEY HARBOUR HOSPITAL: BELLA'S WISHLIST
by Emily Forbes

Single mum Emily gave no-strings-attached surgeon Marco a reason to stay last month:
SYDNEY HARBOUR HOSPITAL: MARCO'S TEMPTATION
by Fiona McArthur

And finally join us this month as Ava and James realise their marriage really is worth saving in
SYDNEY HARBOUR HOSPITAL: AVA'S RE-AWAKENING
by Carol Marinelli

And not forgetting *Sydney Harbour Hospital's* legendary heart surgeon Finn Kennedy. This brooding maverick keeps his women on hospital rotation... But can new doc Evie Lockheart unlock the secrets to his guarded heart? Find out in this enthralling new eight-book continuity from Mills & Boon® Medical Romance™.

A collection impossible to resist!

These books are also available in ebook format from www.millsandboon.co.uk

PROLOGUE

SHE would call him.

Ava Carmichael sat in her office at Sydney Harbour Hospital and stared at her phone, willing herself to pick it up and call her husband. She had just spent the best part of the last hour counselling a couple—telling them to talk, to open up to each other, that if they just forged ahead with communication then things would begin to improve.

As a sexual dysfunction specialist—or sex therapist, as everyone called her—Ava got to say those lines an awful lot.

Well, it was time for the doctor to take her own medicine, Ava decided, reaching out and picking up the phone and dialling in his mobile number. At the last moment she changed her mind, and hung up. She went back to twisting her long dark hair around her fingers—just unsure what it was she should say to him.

That she missed him?

That she was sorry?

Ava didn't know where to start.

Her husband, James, had been away for three months in Brisbane. He had taken a temporary teaching placement at a school of medicine there, which was ridiculous. James was an oncologist and completely hands-on in his work. He loved being with his patients more than anything. Had it been three months of research, it might have made some sense—Sydney Harbour Hospital was cutting-edge and James kept himself right up to date, but James liked reading about findings rather than discovering them. He liked being with his patients and James, her James, wasn't a teacher.

She smiled at the very thought.

The medical students got on his nerves.

He hated explaining his decisions.

He was a man's man, a gorgeous man, her big honest bear of a man who would come home and flake on the sofa sometimes and moan because he wanted it to only be him in the room with his patient, especially when giving bad news.

'It's a teaching hospital,' Ava would point out, lying on the floor, doing her Pilates. 'They have to learn.'

'Yeah, well, how would you like to have a couple of students sitting there watching when you're trying to talk to someone about their bits not working?' There was rather more to her work than that but he'd made a very good point, and he had made her smile too, especially when he checked his own bits were there for a moment, indignant at the very thought.

Well, there *had* been conversations like that one, lovely evenings that had been shared, talking easily about their day, their thoughts, *them*, but those evenings seemed like an awfully long time ago.

Yes, he loved his patients and they loved him back, and the real reason he had taken the position, they both knew, even if they hadn't voiced it, had been because they'd needed space from each other—they'd needed those three months to hopefully sort out their heads.

James and Ava had been married for seven years, but had been together for ever. They had met at university and, quite simply, at the age of eighteen the awkward and rather shy Ava Marwood had discovered love. James had been twenty-one, good-looking, funny and the first person in her life, it seemed, who actually wanted to spend time with her. Like James, she was an only child, but unlike James, who had grown up with parents who adored him, Ava's parents had made no secret she'd been an accident, an inconvenience really. It had been a parade of young nannies who had raised Ava—her parents had been far too busy with their lives, their careers, their endless extra-marital trysts, which, they'd both agreed, kept their relationship alive.

It had been a confusing, lonely childhood and then she had met James and her world had changed. Ava had found a whole new definition for love. It had been completely unexpected, thoroughly reciprocated and though they had their own friends and lives, there was no doubt they had met their match. Everyone thought them the golden couple and it had been golden for a very long while. A thirty-six-year-old James still made her toes curl just looking at him, and he had always made her laugh. And even if he wasn't particularly romantic, it was a love that went so deep Ava had considered it invincible. But over the last two years their marriage had slowly unravelled. With each miscarriage Ava had suffered, they had grown further and further apart and now they were barely talking. In fact, if it weren't for email they would hardly be corresponding at all.

Still fiddling with her hair, she looked at her computer and then went and reread the last email he had sent her.

It was just his flight details really, and all so impersonal it might just as well have come from Admin.

And then, loathing herself, she did it again—checked their bank account with suspicious eyes.

She saw the boutiques he had visited and couldn't quite envision it—James, of all people, in male boutiques!

James, who got a wardrobe update each Christmas and birthday when she went and did it for him, had taken himself off to several trendy shops these past few weeks and from the amount spent he had been having quite a good time of it.

And what was it with all the cash withdrawals?

James never used cash or rarely, but now it was a couple of hundred dollars here, another couple of hundred there, and what was this weekly transfer? A few minutes' research later she found out.

Her husband, who liked nothing better than to lie on the sofa and laugh at her doing her exercises, had, a couple of months ago, gone and joined a gym.

She didn't know if she was being practical or being a fool to believe that James wouldn't cheat. And things must be bad because she was even thinking of turning to her mother for advice!

Call him, Ava counselled herself. *Call him now from your office.* Because each night at home she went to call but couldn't, and each night was spent in tears. Perhaps she could be more upbeat, logical and truthful if she sat at her desk.

More direct.

'Hi.' She kept her voice bright when he answered the phone.

'Ava?' He sounded surprised, well, he would be, she told herself, it was six-twenty in the evening and so rarely did she ring. 'Is everything okay?'

'Of course it is. Does there have to be a problem to ring for a chat?'

'Er...no.'

She could feel his wariness, but she forged on. 'Look, James, I know things haven't been—'

'Ava, can I call you back?' He sounded awkward and James was never awkward. She'd timed the call carefully, knew that he wouldn't be teaching now.

'Is someone there?' she asked, and there was a long silence.

'I'll call you back in ten.'

She sat trying to ignore the unsettled feeling in her stomach that was permanently there these days—he might have a colleague with him, she told herself, but that had never stopped him talking before. They were a very open couple, or had been; he wouldn't give a damn if someone was around—and he wasn't seeing patients so it couldn't be that.

'Sorry about that.' He had called her back five minutes later.

'Why couldn't you talk?'

'Just…' She could almost see his wide shoulders shrugging the way they did when he closed off. 'What did you ring for?'

'Just…' She shrugged her shoulders too.

'Ava.' She could hear his irritation. 'I'm sorry I couldn't talk before, but I can now—you just called at a bad time.'

'Well, when's a good time?' she snapped. 'I called you the other morning and you couldn't talk then either…' He had hardly been able to breathe. More to the point, he'd hardly been able to breathe! She'd rung him at seven and he hadn't answered and she'd called him straight back, and he'd picked up then, trying to pretend he'd been asleep, but he'd been breathless. She knew he was having an affair, except she didn't want to know it. Ava had always thought that their marriage ending was just about them—a private affair, not a real one.

She wasn't stupid. They hadn't slept together since God knows when, more than a year at the very least. As if James wasn't having the time of his life in Brisbane. She was mad to think otherwise.

'Do you want me to order a cake for your mum's birthday?' she asked instead.

'Please.'

'What about a present?'

'I don't know…just think of something.' And that annoyed her too. Veronica Carmichael was a difficult woman; she and Ava had never really got on. A widow, James was her only child, and she was never going to like the woman who, in her eyes, had taken him away and, worse, a woman who couldn't give her grandchildren. Ava had organised a small family gathering for Veronica's sixtieth, which was next weekend, and would on Saturday go out and buy her something lovely for her birthday, something really beautiful. And she'd wrap it too, and then Veronica would unwrap it and thank James, and would go on and on about what a thoughtful son she had when, had it been left to him, there would have been a card bought on the way to her house and no party.

So she and James chatted for another thirty seconds about his flight home on Monday and then she hung up and stared at the view she loved. SHH looked out over Sydney Harbour and the sexual dysfunction centre was on one of the higher floors—the floor was shared with

Psychology and Family Counselling. Nobody would ever get out of the lift otherwise, James sometimes joked when he came up to visit her some lunchtimes, though again, that hadn't happened in a while. Still, every morning that she came into work Ava pinched herself at the view from her window, and she gazed out at it now, to the opera house and the Harbour Bridge, the blue of the ocean and the white sails that dotted it, and she waited for the view to soothe her.

Unfailingly it worked.

It really was a wonderful perk of her job.

It was the same view she looked at the next morning after another tear-filled night when Ginny, her receptionist, came in carrying a huge bunch of flowers from James.

'Ahh…' Ginny beamed and handed her the bouquet. 'He's so romantic.'

Ava *knew* at that point that he was having

an affair. Knew that she wasn't simply being paranoid.

Not once in the seven years they had been married and not even when dating had James sent flowers, not one single time. It just wasn't him. *What do I need to send flowers for?* He'd shrug. *I've done nothing wrong.*

She read the card.

Miss you.

See you on Monday

James x

And she remembered a time, took it out from the back of her memory and polished it till she could clearly see.

It had been two, maybe three years ago.

Yes, three years ago and it had been their wedding anniversary and they'd both decided they were ready to try for a baby. Ava's career had been in a really good place and she'd felt confident she could juggle work and motherhood far better than her mother had. James had bought her a ring, the large amber ring that she was wearing now, because, he'd said, it matched her eyes. And he'd taken her out for dinner, the perfect night, and they'd had the same old good-natured joke as they'd got back to the apartment and she'd moaned about the lack of flowers.

It hurt to remember and she tried not to, but the memory was out there, all polished and gleaming and allowing for total recall.

Tumbling in bed together, making love as they once had.

His big body over hers, his chin all stubbly, those gorgeous green eyes looking down, and she saw in that image what she hadn't seen in a very long time. James was smiling. 'Men only send flowers when they've something to feel guilty about.'

'In your own words, James,' Ava said, and looked at the flowers and wanted to bin them. If her window had opened she would have tossed them out there and then, except her window was sealed closed, and then in came Ginny with a huge vase.

'Put them out in the waiting room,' Ava suggested. 'Let the patients enjoy them.'

'Don't be daft,' Ginny said, and plonked them right there on her desk. 'He sent them for you.'

And there they sat, for appearances sake, their sweet, sickly fragrance filling her nostrils, the violent colours perpetually in her line of vision. She wished they'd just wilt and fade.

Like her marriage.

CHAPTER ONE

'THEY'VE cancelled the surgery.' Ava said nothing for a moment, just stood quietly as her colleague Evie Lockheart leant against the corridor wall, her eyes closed as she struggled to keep in the tears, utterly defeated by what had happened. Ava had seen her walking dazed along the hospital corridor. Even if she didn't know Evie particularly well, she liked her—they had shared the odd conversation and everyone in the hospital knew that Finn Kennedy was having his surgery today.

Complicated surgery that was extremely risky. Ava already knew his operation had been called off—news spread fast around SHH and she couldn't even hazard how Finn must be feeling to have been told an hour before such major surgery that it wasn't going to go ahead.

'It hasn't been cancelled,' Ava said, her voice practical. 'It's been postponed.'

'Well, it might just as well have been cancelled,' Evie said. 'He just told them not to bother booking it again, then he told me to get the hell out.' Evie shook her head. 'I shouldn't be troubling you with this.' She was clearly in distress and not used to sharing her private life, and Ava was more than used to situations like that.

'Come back to my office,' Ava suggested. She could see a couple of nurses turning their heads as they walked past—Evie and Finn were hot topics indeed. Finn was the chief of surgery and a formidable man at best, well known for his filthy attitude and ability to upset the staff, but no one could question his brilliance. His voice could be as cutting as the scalpel he so skilfully wielded, except lately he hadn't been operating and it had done nothing to improve his mood, and today poor Evie was wearing it. 'We can get a coffee there. I'm sure you might like a bit of privacy now.' She walked Evie back along the corridor and to the left and then up in the lifts they went without a word. She walked along the corridor, nodded good morning to Donald, one of the therapists, and then through to her own centre and shook her head when Ginny told her she had a message from the spinal unit.

'I'll call back later,' Ava said. 'I'm not to be disturbed.'

She and Evie entered her office—well, it was more a room. Yes, she had a desk, though it was terribly messy, but the room had a couple of couches and a coffee table, and a small kitchenette where Ava would make her clients a drink, or herself one, if they needed a moment to pause, and she gave Evie that moment now as she went over to make them a drink.

'Finn would never forgive me, you know…' Evie gave a pale smile as she sat down on one of the comfortable couches 'If he knew I was stepping into a sex therapist's office to talk about him.'

'I'd be patronising you if I laughed.' Ava turned around and smiled. 'I hear the same thing I don't know how many times a day. She put on a gruff male voice. '"Well, I never thought I'd find myself here. I really don't need to be here…"' Ava rolled her eyes and poured coffee, taking a little longer than perhaps she needed to, to give Evie a chance to collect herself.

'Well.' Evie gave a wry laugh. 'At least we know that's one type of therapy that Finn doesn't need.'

Ava chose not to correct her—Finn had been using women as sticky plasters for a very long while, there was certainly something going on in that brilliant head of his. Still, that wasn't what Evie needed to hear today. Finn's and her on-again, off-again relationship was clearly taking its toll on her.

'What a view…' Evie noticed her surroundings for the first time. 'Maybe I could ask them to consider moving Emergency up here.'

'The paramedics would never forgive you,' Ava said. 'Do you want me to leave you?' she offered, handing Evie a steaming mug of coffee—Ava wasn't a nosy person at all and she certainly never gossiped. It was why, perhaps, she often found herself in situations such as this one. 'The cleaners have already been in.' She glanced at the desk, wished those blasted flowers were gone, but apart from a couple of wilting roses that the cleaner had removed, they were still there and still taunting her. 'I haven't got any patients for another hour, so you won't be disturbed.'

'No.' Evie shook her head. 'You don't have to

go. It's actually nice to talk, just to be up here and away from the prying eyes.'

'It must be an extra pressure on Finn,' Ava mused. 'Having to have his operation where he's the chief of surgery. Still, there's no better place.' SHH was the best hospital for this sort of procedure, there was no question that it might be done elsewhere. It was experimental and even with the best surgery, the best equipment, there were no guarantees that Finn's ability to operate again could be saved. Indeed, there was a good chance that he would be left a quadriplegic.

Ava knew that, not because of the gossip that was flying around the hospital but because, unbeknown to Evie, Finn had actually been in for mandatory counselling prior to surgery. The team had discussed who should see him and Ava had immediately declined. She didn't know Finn particularly well, but they lived in the same apartment block, Kirribilli Views—

his penthouse apartment was directly above hers—and though they barely greeted each other if they met on the stairs or in the lift, still, it could surely only make things more awkward for Finn.

He'd seen Donald instead.

And even though Donald was terribly experienced—he did both family counselling and sexual dysfunction and his patients adored him—Ava wondered if his brusque approach would mesh with Finn in such a delicate matter.

Ava dealt with spinal patients a lot. Her work gave her much pleasure, seeing relationships saved, helping people to learn that there could be life, a satisfying sex life even, after such catastrophic events. Her work was, in fact, moving more towards trauma and post-traumatic stress disorder patients, it was how she and Evie had first started talking. Evie worked in Accident and Emergency and had dropped by for a chat about a 'patient'. Ava was sure, quite sure, that the person they had been discussing was Finn. Finn's brother had been a soldier like Finn. His brother had died in Finn's arms and shrapnel from the bomb that had killed his brother was still lodged in Finn's neck, and it was that that was causing his health issues.

Sometimes Ava wondered if Finn had ever heard the rows between her and James, not that there had been many, really, before he'd gone away to Brisbane. They had been so deep into injury time by then that she and James hadn't talked much at all, but Finn had never intruded, there had been no chatting on the stairs or anything, just a very occasional 'Good morning'. And not once had Finn questioned her about her red, swollen eyes, neither had he done the neighbourly thing and popped around to see if she was okay when she'd lost the last baby. Ava cringed at the memory—Finn had been in the lift that day—the cramping had started on her way home and she had just wanted to get into her apartment, to call her doctor, to lie down, but there had been this awful sudden gush and then a crippling, bend-over pain and, terribly practical, Finn had helped her to her door, had taken her inside and had then called James. They'd never discussed it further—instead it had been a brief nod in passing and Ava had been grateful for that. Grateful now that Finn never stopped to ask when James was returning, or how she was getting on.

No, they just shared the same brief nod and greeting.

Grief recognising grief perhaps.

Respecting it.

Avoiding it.

'I can't believe we're going to have to go through all this again.' Evie broke into her thoughts. 'I really don't think he'll consent to surgery a second time.'

'Why did they cancel the operation?' Ava

asked. 'I thought they had everyone on board, it's been planned for weeks.'

'This piece of equipment they need,' Evie explained, 'they're having trouble calibrating it. There's a technician coming over from America so it looks like it will be another week before the surgery can go ahead. They just can't risk even a single mistake.'

'What did he say when they told him?'

'Not much—a few choice words and then he took out his drip, put on his suit, told me where to go, and not very nicely either, and now he's back at work—he's doing a ward round as we speak, no doubt chewing out everybody in his path. Ava…' Evie's eyes were anguished '…the thing is, with Finn and I, I know it's very on-and-off, I know how appalling he can be, but in the last few days we've been close. Last night we…' She let out a startled half-laugh. 'I can't believe I'm discussing this.'

'You won't make me blush,' Ava said.

'We had a really nice night.' Evie was awkward. 'I mean, it was really intimate, amazing. It wasn't just sex, it was so tender, we were so close.' Ava said nothing, reminded herself she was thinking as a friend, not a therapist, and she let Evie continue. 'And now, just like that, he's told me to get out, that he doesn't want me around.'

'Give him some time,' Ava said. 'He would have been building himself up for this surgery, and to have it cancelled at the last minute—'

'But cancellations happen all the time and you don't see couples breaking up over it,' Evie interrupted. 'He said that now he knows a bit how the patients feel when we cancel them at the last minute.'

'Ooh, are we going to get a new, compassionate Finn?' Ava was pleased to see Evie smile. A cheerful person, Ava found that a little dose of humour helped in most situations.

Most, not all.

'Finn compassionate?' Evie rolled her eyes, and then sat quietly as she finished her drink. Ava sat in silence too, a comfortable silence that was perhaps needed by Evie before she headed back out there, but after a moment or two in their own worlds it was time to resume appearances, to play their parts. Evie drained her drink and stood. 'Thanks so much, Ava.'

'Any time,' Ava said.

'Oh.' Evie suddenly remembered. 'That gorgeous husband of yours comes back today, doesn't he?'

'This morning.' Ava nodded. 'He's heading straight in to work. That's James.'

'Well, you can see him tonight,' Evie said. 'He's the luckiest guy in the world, isn't he? Married to a sex therapist…'

Ava grinned. 'Again, I'd be patronising you if I laughed, if you had any idea of the amount of times I hear that each day…'

She was *sick* of hearing it.

So too must James be.

The assumption that they must have most amazing sex life and wonderful relationship was a pressure in itself. As if people thought her job followed her home, as if the smiling, cheerful, practical Ava, who was open to discuss everything, who managed to deal with the most sensitive subjects with barely a blink, translated to the Ava at home.

Finn would never say such a thing, Ava thought as she saw Evie out.

Or maybe he would, she mused—nervous, embarrassed, new to a wheelchair, maybe Finn would crack the same old jokes if she offered her help.

She stood alone in her office and looked out the window at the glittering view and wondered if she could stand to leave it, not so much the view but her work here. She didn't want to start over at another hospital or open a private practice. Because SHH was so cutting-edge she got the patients in her office that she was most interested in helping. It was no doubt the same reason James would remain here, but how hard would it be to work in the same hospital, to see your ex-husband most days?

Ex-husband.

There, she'd said it and she didn't like how it sounded.

More than that, she didn't want to be James's ex-wife.

CHAPTER TWO

'LOVELY flowers.' Elise was a bit flustered but George was friendlier this time. 'From your husband?'

'They are.' Ava smiled. 'Come in, take a seat.'

She had been seeing them for a few months now. For George and Elise it was a complicated process and not as simple as writing a prescription. George had been in an accident at work last year, an appalling accident where he'd seen a colleague die. It wasn't just George's physical injuries that had caused him pain. Over and over he had relived the moment of the accident and the depression and anxiety had been all-engulfing. He'd seen his GP but the medication for the depression had affected his libido, which had increased his anxiety, and by the time they had arrived at Ava's, the pair had all but given up, not just on their sex life but on themselves.

She was seeing them monthly as a couple and George was also having one-on-one counselling with Ava, but more about the accident and the flashbacks he was getting and his appalling guilt that the colleague who had died had been so much younger than him.

'How have you two been?' Ava asked.

'We're doing fine,' George said, handing over a folder. 'I've done my homework.'

Ava grinned and checked off their sheets. Her methods were a bit flaky at times, and with some couples she made things a bit more fun. With George and Elise she had them playing Scrabble, taking walks, doing little quizzes to find out more about each other, just little things, and she looked through the sheets.

'Elise?' She saw the woman's worried expression as she handed over a folder. She looked as if she was about to start to cry. 'Elise, the homework's for fun…'

'It's not that.' She was really flustered, Ava realised. 'You know you said we weren't to…' She could hardly say it.

'I suggested that you didn't try to have sex.'

To take the pressure off George Ava had suggested a sex ban, kissing and holding hands only—which apparently they hadn't done for decades.

'Oh, we haven't,' Elise assured her.

'Okay.'

'We did get a bit carried away, though,' George admitted.

Quite a bit carried away, it turned out! By the time their hour was up, they were all smiling. 'I'll see you again next month and, George, you in two weeks,' she said to the couple. 'And follow the rules this time.'

She grinned at her own success. Okay, they had a long way to go, but they were both determined to get there, and with a couple as lovely as them, they would, Ava was quite sure.

'Ava?' She heard a knock at the same time she heard her name, Elise and George had left the door open. She felt her stomach tighten at the sound of her husband's voice, and she turned round.

'James.' There he stood, tall, strong, gorgeous and *different*. His light brown hair, which usually fell rumpled and messy, now had a modern cut, and usually his chin was crying out for a razor, but he was clean-shaven today. Generally James wore jeans and a T-shirt or jumper, depending on the season. His patients, he'd explain, had more on their minds than whether or not the doctor was wearing a suit—but now and then he donned one and when he did, he quite simply took her breath away.

He wasn't wearing a suit today but, dressed in grey linen trousers and a black fitted shirt, he was a mixture between the two versions of James she adored and it almost killed her to see it. James never bought himself new clothes; they simply didn't interest him. Her heart stopped in her chest for a moment, seeing him in new attire, wondering who had bought them for him, or who James had bought them to impress. She had a horrible glimpse into her future if they both worked at SHH, watching the man she loved and knew so well change before her eyes.

'You've lost weight,' she said, because he had. He was a big man, and had never been *that* overweight, but he'd lost a lot and now stood broad, lean and toned.

'A bit.' He shrugged.

'How was your flight?' How stilted and formal she sounded when really she wanted to run to him, to rest her head on his chest, to welcome him home, to say how much she had missed him, except she greeted him like a colleague and clearly it was noticed, because he didn't even answer the question, just shot her a slightly incredulous look that that was all she had to say after his three months away.

'I'll see you tonight,' James said instead, and then as he turned to go, he stopped. 'Ava, we need to talk.'

He'd been saying that for months—no, years—as more and more she'd shut him out, only this time it was a different conversation to be had. 'I know we do.'

'I'll speak to you tonight.' He didn't come over and kiss her, he just turned and walked away and headed out to work, to involve himself in his patients. Only it wasn't his familiar scent that lingered. Instead she smelt cologne. Ava wished she had patients scheduled this morning, that she could think about someone else's problems instead of her own.

Instead, she was giving a lecture.

She had her little case packed, filled with aids that would make the student nurses laugh at first, but she would push through it, hoping to get her message across, hoping that one day in the future her words would be recalled and a sensitive, informed word might be had by one of them to a patient, that there was help available.

Except she felt a fraud as she stood there, this cheerful, laughing, sexual dysfunction specialist married to the gorgeous James.

She couldn't remember the last time that they had slept together and wasn't stupid enough to think in the three months he'd been away, in the years they'd been away from each other physically, that James wouldn't have seen someone else.

Someone he liked enough to lose weight for, to tone up for, to buy new clothes for and splash on cologne for—it wasn't the James she knew. She knew that she'd lost him long ago.

Lost them.

CHAPTER THREE

'LOOK at you!'

The reception that greeted him as he walked onto the unit for the first time in three months was far more friendly and receptive than Ava's had been.

'Where did you disappear to?' Carla, the unit manager on the day ward, asked.

'Brisbane,' James said.

'She meant this.' Harriet gave a friendly sort of pat to his stomach as she walked past and, yes, he'd forgotten that Harriet had been getting a bit too friendly before he'd gone away.

'Ava's got herself a whole new man,' Carla said, and winked at him, and he grinned back, because Carla would soon have a word if needed. 'Bet she's delighted to have you back.'

'She is,' James said, and as Harriet pulled on her gloves he watched her cheeks flood with colour as he made things clear. 'And I'm really glad to be back—I've just been up to see her.'

He'd read through files and results and it really was good to be back—at least on the unit. He tried not to think about Ava's lukewarm—or, rather, stone-cold—reception. A long breath came out of his nose as he tried not to think about it but, hell, he'd thought she might be at the airport, he'd even emailed his flight times as a prompt, and then when she hadn't been he had stopped by the flat, just in case she'd taken the morning off, but of course she was at work.

'We've a new patient this morning.' Carla handed him a file. 'Richard Edwards. He was supposed to be in on Friday for his first round of chemotherapy but he cancelled. I wondered if you could have a word with him as he's ever so anxious. Wouldn't be surprised if he refuses again.'

'Sure.' James read through the file and his colleague Blake's meticulous notes. Richard was nineteen and had been recently diagnosed with testicular cancer. He was stage one and all his markers were good, but after discussion with Blake he had decided to go ahead with chemotherapy, though he was clearly wavering on that decision now.

'Where is he?'

'He's in the coffee room. Do you want me to bring him through to your office?'

'I'll find him.'

James headed down to the patients' and relatives' coffee room and met with the young man and his worried parents. 'I'll have a chat with Richard…'

'We'll come,' his anxious parents said, but James shook his head.

'I'll speak with you all shortly, but first I'd like to speak with Richard himself.'

'He gets overwhelmed—'

'I'm sure he does,' James said. 'That's why I'll go through everything again afterwards.'

'Thanks for that,' Richard said as they took a seat in James's office. 'They've been great and everything, but…' He struggled to finish his sentence and James tried for him.

'They're not the ones going through it?'

Richard nodded. 'They don't understand why I wouldn't want the chemotherapy if it gives you more chance that it won't come back. Blake seemed to think it was the better option, but he did speak about waiting and watching,' Richard said. 'I've just started a new job, I've got a new girlfriend and she's been great and everything, but I just can't imagine…' He closed his eyes for a moment and James didn't interrupt. 'I always look after myself. I'm a vegetarian. I just think I might be able to take care of this myself. I've been looking into things…'

'It's called watchful waiting,' James said. 'There's no evidence your cancer has spread so if you adopt that approach then you'll come back regularly for tests—and if it does come back the treatment is still there for you. Some people prefer that, whereas others find it far more stressful and just want the treatment straight away.' He spent time with Richard, going through everything, giving him pointers to do his own research, and it was good to be back at work with real patients. He liked informing his patients, liked them informed, and Richard was. He didn't, at this stage, want to go ahead with the treatment, but as they wound up the discussion, along came the question, the one he was asked so many times. 'What would you do if it was you?' There were variations to the question, of course—if it was your wife, your mother, your daughter, your son. So often James was asked what he would do in their place, and normally he answered it easily, but maybe he was out of practice, because he hesitated a moment before answering.

'What you're doing,' James said. 'I'd weigh up my options. Do you want to make another appointment so we can talk again in a couple of weeks?

'That would be great,' Richard said. 'Will you speak with my parents?'

'Sure.'

It didn't go down very well, but James took his time with them too, assuring them that it was a valid option, that Richard wasn't closing any doors—and sometimes, James thought as he headed back to the treatment area, it was the relatives who had the hardest time dealing with things.

'No go?' Carla asked.

'Not at this stage,' James said. 'I've given him some decent sites to look at and some reading material.'

As he wrote in Richard's notes James could fully understand Richard's decision. He was fortunate that he did have options, and chemotherapy wasn't a decision to be made lightly, or pressured into. He looked through the glass screen at the patients in for treatment this morning and recognised a couple of them.

There was Georgia, back to do battle again, her headphones on. She gave him a smile as she caught him looking over and James returned it, and then he let her be because she closed her eyes and went back to the affirmations she played through the headphones each time her treatment was delivered. Then he looked over at Heath, who didn't look over or up. He was still too busy controlling the world from his laptop, still insisting the world wouldn't survive without him for a couple of days…

It just might have to, though.

James must have dropped his suitcase off on his way to the hospital because when Ava walked into the apartment, laden with bags, there it was in the lounge.

She could smell that blasted cologne in the air, just a trace that lingered, and she opened a window to let in some fresh air. They had a two-bedroom apartment at Kirribilli Views. It was the perfect place for a young professional couple and several other medical staff from the hospital lived there. One of the bedrooms was used as James's study. Many times while he had been away Ava had found herself in there and she found herself in there now. It was always messy. James had forbidden her from tidying it, insisting he knew where everything was. There was their wedding photo on the desk and Ava couldn't help but think how young and happy they looked. She wandered into their bedroom—well, for the last year or so it had been her bedroom. She kept her home far neater than she kept her office, though it was hard to keep anything tidy with James around, even though they had Gladys, the cleaner, coming once a week. Really, for the last three months Gladys must've thought herself on holiday—well, she'd get a shock when she came in this week now that James was back.

She wandered into their en suite. Gladys would have a fit when she saw it, because for the last three months it had been spotless. Ava routinely wiped down the shower after use and folded towels and put them back. James left his clothes where they dropped and his towels too. Funny, that even though he slept on the sofa, he always used the en suite. There was a small bathroom in the hallway, a guest bathroom, and James probably didn't want to be a guest in his own home.

God, she was nervous, and she jumped when her phone bleeped a text from James telling her he'd be home about seven.

Well, he wasn't exactly racing home his first night back.

So she put the shopping away and marinated some chicken and tried to tell herself it was ridiculous to feel so nervous. It was just James coming home.

'Sorry about that.' She jumped as she heard James's key in the door. 'I dropped into Mum's.' He was balancing containers of food from Veronica, who seemed to think he needed rations to fortify him. He gave her a kiss but he was still holding the containers, so it was rather hit-and-miss.

'No problem.' Ava was used to him being late, so she didn't put the vegetable steamer on till she heard him come through the door. 'Dinner won't be long.' It felt strange to be cooking for two again. The last three months she'd been eating mainly frozen meals, healthy ones, though, and with extra steamed vegetables, and she'd taken up exercising again and lost a little bit of weight too. Still, cooking for two really meant cooking for two in this house. James liked jacket potatoes and butter with *everything* and he hated steamed vegetables, which were what Ava liked. She'd started eating really healthily when she'd lost the first baby, and she couldn't quite let go of it, but she *was* trying to get her old self back.

'Do you want veggies?' she asked as she served up, and he gave her the oddest look. 'I mean, you've lost weight, I thought maybe you're on a diet.'

'I joined a gym.' James shrugged. 'I can eat what I want now,' he said. 'It's great.'

No, she wanted to correct him, because it wasn't just about that, but she didn't want to start the night with nagging. She'd already pursed her lips when he'd come home with cartons of chicken and stir-fried rice from his mum's.

'You look like you've lost weight too.' James followed her into the living area and they sat down at the table for the first time in a very long time. She felt more awkward than one of her patients on their first visit. 'I've been riding,' Ava said, 'and swimming.'

'That's good,' James said. 'That's good, Ava.'

It was good, except she felt as if she was giving up on her dream… She'd given up so many things trying to hold on to their baby. Their first pregnancy the doctor had said that of course she could ride, given that she regularly did, and she was incredibly fit after all. So she'd carried on riding and swimming each morning and they had made love lots, as they always had.

The second pregnancy, she'd given up riding, figuring that it seemed stupid to risk a fall.

The third pregnancy, she had felt as if she were on a tightrope and had given up swimming, and by the fourth she had given up James.

And when she'd lost that one, Ava simply knew she couldn't go through it again. It had been a relief to go on the Pill, to decide that children weren't going to happen for them, to get on with their lives.

Except they hadn't.

She sliced her grilled chicken, tried not to think about it. She didn't want to think about babies. It was hard not to, though. She never had any problems getting pregnant. It was staying pregnant that had proved impossible. Six weeks, nine weeks, seven weeks and then ten weeks once…

She remembered Finn dragging her to the door.

Remembered his voice as he'd called her husband, but by then it had already been too late.

'So what did you get up to in Brisbane?'

'Not much. The teaching was pretty full on.'

'You seemed pretty busy.'

He stood to get another bottle of water.

'Might treat myself to sparkling,' James said, and she knew it was a dig, because after three months apart they should be popping corks.

'Can you check I turned the oven off?' She watched his shoulders stiffen, knew it drove him crazy when once it had made him laugh, but she was forever checking things like that.

'Well?'

'It's off,' he said, cracking open the sparkling water, filling his glass and then raising it. 'Cheers!'

She was quite sure he hadn't checked but didn't say so, very determined not to start a row.

Or face *that* conversation.

'I got you Mum's present for her birthday.' God, but it was awkward. They hadn't seen each other for three months so they should be at it over the table right now, completely unable to keep their hands off each other. Instead, there had been no contact and, worse, the conversation was strained. They simply had nothing to say to each other—it was worse than a first date.

'How's your work?' James asked.

'Busy.'

'I heard about Finn's operation being cancelled.'

'Postponed.'

'Ava.' He'd finished his chicken and she had barely started hers. 'While I've been away, I've been—'

'I had a chat with Evie…' They didn't speak at the same time. James started and she interrupted and then stopped. 'Sorry.' She knew she had to face it. 'You were saying?'

'It can wait,' James said, because he didn't want to face it either. 'How was Evie?'

They watched a movie, or tried to, but it was a crime one and she hated those, so midway through Ava gave up and went on her computer, writing up patient notes, fixing other people's lives instead of her own.

'I'm going to bed.' She didn't bend her head to kiss him and James hardly looked up, neither quite brave enough to have *that* talk.

He sat in the semi-darkness, teeth gritted, and tried to concentrate on the film, because if he didn't he might just march into that bedroom and say something he'd regret.

Some welcome home.

He was a night person, and once Ava had been. She'd been a morning person too—up at the crack of dawn and swimming on weekdays, riding at weekends, and he was glad she was doing that again. It was the early nights he couldn't stand and she was going to bed even earlier. Now it was lights down at ten, like some school trip.

James hauled himself from the sofa and wandered into his study, saw the wedding photo on the desk and he barely recognised them so he closed the door, went back into the living room, opened up his case then headed to the cupboard and took out a blanket and pillow and tossed them down.

God, but he hated that sofa.

There was a small bathroom in the hall and he was quite sure she'd prefer that he use it, but he refused to, so he took out his toiletry bag from the case and walked into the bedroom where she lay pretending to be asleep as he went into the en suite.

James took off the shirt and discarded the linen pants on the floor, then he rinsed off the cologne and looked at her make-up bag, saw the little packet of pills that was supposed to have been the solution. He thought about having a shower, but decided that it could wait till morning. There was a show he liked starting soon, so he put a towel around his hips and walked past her bed on the way to the sofa.

They'd talk tomorrow, he decided, or maybe they should wait till after his mum's birthday. He was starving. One piece of grilled chicken and a baby potato with a tiny knob of low-fat sour cream—there hadn't been butter in the apartment for years, another thing that was banned. Maybe he should ring for a pizza; that would really get under her skin…

And then he stopped.

He just stopped.

Because he could do this no longer, because it had come to *this*. He was sick of the sofa and sick of not wanting to come home—and, as hard as it was, he had to say it—he was an oncologist after all, should be able to stand by a bed and deliver a grim diagnosis.

'Ava.' He stood by the bed. 'I need to talk to you.' Her eyes were still closed but he carried on. 'These last months while I've been away in Brisbane, I've been doing a lot of thinking.'

'James.' She turned on her side. 'It's late, can

we talk tomorrow? At the weekend maybe?' She didn't want to hear it.

'No,' James said. 'We're going to talk now. You know how we agreed about no children, that we weren't going to have babies...'

She didn't want this conversation, just didn't want to have it, but James pressed on regardless. 'When you went on the Pill, I thought it was supposed to take the pressure off, supposed to be a relief, but if anything it's made things worse.' She could feel him standing over her, could feel tears building behind her eyes, and then as he carried on, she grew angry. 'I mean, even if we only had sex because you wanted to get pregnant, at least we did it...'

'Oh, poor James.' She opened her eyes now—angry eyes that met his. Three months apart and a whole lot of thinking and that was all he could come up with, that they weren't doing *it* any more. 'So you're not getting enough!'

'I know I'm not good at this.' James hissed

his frustration. 'I know that I say the wrong thing, but will you just hear me out? Every day you tell your patients to talk things through,' James said. 'Every night you come home and refuse to.'

'What do you want to talk about, James? That we're not doing *it*? Well, sorry…' And she stopped. She just didn't have the energy to argue any more, couldn't drag up any more excuses, and she sat up in the bed and looked at the face she had always loved, and he was looking at her as if he didn't even know who she was.

'We're finished, aren't we?' James said it for them and it made her want to retch, but instead she just sat there as he answered the question for them. 'I mean, how much more finished can you be if after being away for three months I'm automatically heading for the sofa?'

'Some sex therapist!' She made the stupid joke for him, the one he must hear every day, when no doubt people nudged him and said how lucky he was. If only they knew. She wanted to reach out to him but she didn't know how. She'd tried so many times to have the conversations that ran in her head with him, to mourn the loss of their babies together. She had tried to tell him how she was feeling, that it wasn't just the baby she grieved for but the chance to be a mother, to fix what had been broken with her own mum. She really had tried. At first she'd cried on him. James all big and strong, telling her things would be fine, that there would be other babies, except that wasn't what she had wanted him to say.

Neither had it helped when he'd told her that they'd try again soon because she hadn't wanted him to say that either.

He was an oncologist, for God's sake; he should know how to handle grief!

She could remember how excited he had been the first time she had been pregnant. He'd told her how much he wanted children, how much he was looking forward to being a dad. He'd shared his dreams with her and she felt like she'd ended them.

'What happens now?' She looked over at him.

'I don't know,' James admitted. 'I guess we both get a lawyer.'

'We don't need lawyers.'

'That's what everyone says, isn't it?' James said. 'Let's just get a lawyer and get it done.'

He headed out to the sofa and she called him back. 'It's your mum's birthday next week-end—should we do it after that?'

He gave a short nod. 'I'll go to a hotel tomorrow. I'll tell her after, well, not straight after…'

'Okay.' She couldn't stand it—she couldn't stand to look at what she was losing so she moved to turn out the bedside light. 'Night, then.'

That incensed him. He strode over, his face

suddenly livid, and as she plunged them into darkness he turned the light back on and stood over her. 'You can't even squeeze out a tear, can you?' James accused.

'Don't say that.' Because if she started crying she thought she might never stop.

'You're just glad it's done, aren't you?' James said. 'Well, you know what? So am I. It's been hell…'

'It wasn't all bad.'

'No, Ava, it wasn't all bad,' James said, his voice rising, 'but it wasn't all good either, so don't try and sugarcoat the situation. This last year has been hell and I just want done with it.' She winced at his anger, at the hurt that was there, and then he stopped shouting. 'Sorry.' he ran a hand through his hair. 'I'm sorry, okay? I don't want to fight.' He sat down on the bed and took her hand. 'We'll do this civilly. I don't want any more rows, we'll finish things nicely… You're right, it wasn't all bad.'

And he looked at her. 'There was an awful lot of good.'

'I don't want to fight,' she begged, because she hated fights, she hated rows, they made her feel ill, and James knew that.

'We won't,' he promised. 'We'll just…' He gave a shrug. She could see all his muscles, he'd really toned up, he looked amazing, he felt amazing on her skin as his hand met her arm. 'We'll remember the good times,' James said. 'We don't want to end up like Donna and Neil.'

And they both shared a pale laugh, because they'd had Donna and Neil over many times, at first together and then, when their marriage had broken up, separately, where they'd sat bitching and moaning about their exes—and James and Ava had shared many cross-eyed looks in the kitchen as they'd topped up drinks or put out dips…

'"He makes out he's so easygoing…"' She put on Donna's voice.

'"Don't know what she spends it on."' He put on Neil's.

'"He was crap in bed…"' She was still Donna.

'Well, you won't be saying that,' James said, but in his own voice now.

'No,' she admitted. 'Though you might.'

'No,' James said, and he smiled. ''Cos when we were good…' She knew what was happening as he leant over, she knew what she was doing as she put her hand to the chest that was so very close, and she didn't push him away this time, but felt his skin beneath her fingers, and her fingers lingered as she returned his kiss. She knew it wasn't a last-ditch effort to save a relationship, it was a kiss goodbye, and sex because you never would again.

She thought about it quite logically as for the first time in a year their mouths met properly, so logically for a moment that she knew it had been the same for Finn and Evie, the wonderful night Evie had recalled had been goodbye sex from Finn—while he still could.

Goodbye sex where you tried to imprint every detail as you kissed the other goodbye.

And logic went then.

His mouth was the same as the one she'd first kissed at uni, and his chin was a little stubbly now, not smooth as it had been this morning. God, but she'd loved his mouth. His shoulders were broader too, she thought as her fingers traced them, and she loved the solidness of him, loved the new toned James beneath her hands, and she pulled him further into her. And even if they hadn't been together in a very long time, still their bodies knew and recognised each other, still they matched the other's wants, a delicious familiarity, and she didn't care if he'd been with another, because she'd got to love him first.

She'd started wearing pyjamas in their year apart, big, baggy things that were buttoned to the neck, and James very slowly took them off. He looked at her body, which was way too slender now, but he had loved it for more than its shape and he kissed her ever harder.

Even if he'd lost weight he was still big, big and strong. He pressed her into the pillow and pulled the sheet down as he kissed her deeper till his towel was long gone and he was over her and here she could cry, his mouth on her salty cheeks as he slipped inside and moved inside where only he had ever been. She remembered the first time as their bodies meshed for the last time. She remembered so many times. Their first kiss on the beach, the night in his room when they had first made love, a carousel of images that flashed through her mind, and they flashed through his too—the first time, how many hours, days, weeks it had taken her to unbend, to give in to him, and the bliss he had felt when she had. He told her with words and with moans how good it felt to be there.

They had always been noisy, James the most, just a delicious, uninhibited lover, and she'd miss their sounds, miss the one she was making now as her body throbbed its admission as to how much she had missed him. He moaned as he came—a deep, loud moan with her name on the end of it—and she'd miss that too, and then they lay there, conjoined, neither speaking for a while, till he rolled off and lay looking up at the ceiling, waiting for the carousel to slow down.

'Well,' Ava said finally, 'that was very civil.'

'Yeah, I can be sometimes.'

She curled up into a ball and faced away from him, wondered if he would head to the couch now, but he pulled her over to him, tucked her right into him and shielded her through their last night.

She woke to the dark, as she often did, and wriggled from his arms and lay on her back, trying to sort out problems in her head—sometimes she laughed out loud as she sorted them, but she wasn't laughing this morning; instead, she lay there fearing the dawn.

He hated the clock. He hit the snooze button, then thought better of it, leant over and turned it off. He climbed out of bed and headed to the shower. His toiletry bag from his time away was still unpacked and he went to get the razor, but couldn't be bothered. He'd only have to pack it again, so he went into the shower instead.

Maybe they could make it. Maybe after last night now they could somehow talk. He was supposed to be packing a bag and leaving for a hotel, except for the first time in more than a year there was a glimmer of hope. Yes, he knew last night hadn't been about rekindling them but somehow it felt as if they had. He thought of her body and how it had responded to him as he washed himself, thought of her warm and half-asleep in the bed just a few steps away from him, wondered about going back to her, just sliding in beside her still wet from the shower. He was hardening just thinking of her. Maybe, James thought, they should just talk; maybe they should just get angry and have a row. He knew how much she hated them, but maybe they should just shout it out, or maybe he should go in and just… He decided otherwise. It wouldn't be particularly sensitive to go in there and try to save his marriage with a throbbing hard-on, so instead of shower gel he picked up her conditioner and lathered himself with the scent of her, because that was what he often did, then bit down on his lip so as not to call out to her—when a couple of years ago he would have.

'Hey, sex therapist,' he'd used to call out from the shower, 'I've got a bit of a problem here…'

He leant his head on his arm against the shower wall as he recalled it, how she'd slipped into to the shower to 'take a closer look'. He remembered the time, before babies and miscarriages and depression and hell, his hand moving faster and the carousel was back and spinning faster now. He backed against the wall, using both hands now, remembering her hands cupping… And then he stopped.

Everything just stopped for a moment.

Even the water seemed to, because it all just seemed to go still and silent till his senses returned again and he could hear the cascade of the water, and could feel the lump in his hand. He tried to detach, to examine it clinically, and he almost managed to—could feel the lump that was certainly suspicious, except now there was no clinical detachment, he could feel sweat running down his head too, running down his back, and it wasn't the water…it was the cold sweat of fear.

'James?' He heard her voice and looked up. He heard the concern in her voice too, and

Ava was far too open-minded to care what he got up to in the shower, and in that moment she knew.

CHAPTER FOUR

'I DON'T need to leave a specimen,' James said. 'I'm not exactly in the mood.'

'Well, you'd better get yourself in the mood,' Donald said brusquely. 'Of course you will still have one testicle, but if you need chemotherapy…'

'We both decided ages ago that we're not having children.'

'James.' Donald was always blunt. He had a completely different approach from Ava. She sat there beside James for the counselling session that the surgical oncologist had insisted on, and she didn't like being on the other end of it. Ava wanted to get the hell out. 'Your marriage is over.' He looked over at Ava, who sat with her face rigid. 'You've pretty much said that you're just together for appearances' sake.'

'We didn't say that,' Ava snapped. In fact, it had been James who had said it almost the moment they'd sat down, had told Donald straight that their marriage was finished, had said up front that he didn't even know why Ava was in there with him.

'You wouldn't be here if I didn't have cancer,' James said. 'I'd be in a lawyer's office now and so would you.'

'Well, in here you can forget appearances' sake. You wanted to put off this operation so you didn't ruin your mother's birthday—for God's sake, man!'

It was Thursday. James had already had a battery of tests and there were more still to come. Blake was the oncologist that James had chosen for his treatment, thought it would be the surgical oncologist doing the operation tomorrow. He would have his testicle out, and a nice prosthetic one put in. There was one on Donald's desk now, like a strange worry ball, and she was sorely tempted to squeeze it now, though she had handed it straight to James like a hot coal when Donald had first passed it, like some bizarre game of pass the parcel. James had given it a very cursory squeeze and put it back on the desk and they both sat trying to ignore that little saline-filled ball. Ava stared out the window instead, at a view that had once soothed, as Donald spoke on.

'It's often a very treatable cancer. You may well recover from this—have the two of you thought about that? Have you, James?' Donald asked. 'Have you even let yourself consider a wonderful future, one in which you're well—where you meet someone else and fall in love and you both want to have children?'

Ava felt as if she was choking. She had this sudden vision of James running around the garden in the house they'd intended to buy when they had children. They'd wanted a weatherboard and hopefully one with a massive garden.

'Three bedrooms,' she'd said as they'd looked through the real-estate pages.

'No, four.' He'd kissed her, patting her belly because they'd wanted loads of kids. They'd put the flat at Kirribilli on the market when she'd first got pregnant and had then wandered around homes trying to choose the one that would suit their family. She could see it in her mind's eye now, a gorgeous old weatherboard and loads of white iceberg roses and wisteria too—could see James running around the garden, clearly at one with his saline ball, children hanging off him as she trudged past on her way back from the shops, with her frozen healthy meals for one and a tin of cat food.

She hated it that he took the specimen jar.

They walked down the long corridor, James with the jar and pathology slip, and he was shown to a room. She didn't kiss his rigid, tense face, neither did she offer him a *hand.* Instead, she just stood there.

'I'll be in in the morning to see you.'

'There's no need to come in,' James said. 'It's a very simple procedure…'

'Your mum will be there,' Ava said. 'It will look strange if I'm not.' She wanted to be there, she wanted him home with her tonight, not checked into the hospital because he was first on the list and he wanted the bliss of a sleeping pill.

'James, please,' Ava said, 'please, can we talk?'

'Talk?' He gave an incredulous laugh, 'That's the one thing we don't do, remember? Or rather one of the many things we don't do.'

And he walked into the room with the specimen jar that would soon hold his future and it terrified her that he might have one. Of course she wanted a future for James but she wanted it to be with her. Ava wanted to walk into the room and be with him now, wanted to make this hell somehow easier for him, but instead she had to head for home.

Her head was pounding, it really was.

Every root in her scalp throbbed a pulse. They'd been together so long every step was a memory.

It was here she'd started to lose the last pregnancy. That first low cramp that she'd tried to ignore and pretend hadn't happened and then a block later she'd got the next.

The sun was hot and her blouse clung to her and home just seemed too far, and she didn't want to retrace her footsteps so she walked into Pete's instead, but it was a place she and James had often gone together, and it had been ages since Ava had been there. She sat at a table and ordered a glass of sparkling water and rummaged in her bag for some headache pills, but of course she had none.

'Ava!' She heard her name called but she ignored it, and there must have been something on her face that told people to stay away, because no one came over. Pete's was filled with hospital personnel. It was a place where many met. She couldn't face going up to the bar and seeing anyone so she sat alone at her table and looked out of the window, watching all the people walking past, just getting on with their day as if it was just another day, except her marriage was ending and James had cancer and she wanted to be with her husband so badly that even the phone ringing felt like an invasion.

She answered her phone. 'He's fine, Veronica. He said he doesn't want visitors tonight.' She did her best to answer her mother-in-law's endless questions, but Veronica wasn't just a nosy old boot, she was a perceptive one too.

'It's because he's a doctor,' Ava said, when Veronica pointed out that these days people went in in the morning and James had told her it was a day-case procedure and nothing to worry about. 'They're just doing him a favour so he can get a bit more sleep. He'll have a sleeping tablet and be knocked out. It's better than him being at home, stressing.'

Except James didn't stress.

It was one of the things she had so loved about him. Arrogant, some said; male chauvinist, a few others, but he wasn't—he was just this big bull of a male and she loved him for it. This man who didn't sweat the small stuff, who didn't care about clothes and flowers, and it wasn't that he expected her to do the washing-up: he'd happily leave it undone.

'Can I get you anything else?' She blinked as she saw the waiter taking away her empty glass. She couldn't remember even drinking the sparkling water.

'A glass of wine,' Ava replied, and then she had to go through whether she wanted red or white. She stabbed her finger at a random one on the menu. She didn't care what she had, she simply couldn't face going back to the flat, to lie in bed without him.

But they had been sleeping apart for months, Ava reminded herself as the waiter came back. She sipped on her drink.

'Ava!' It was Mia and Luca walking into the bar, friends they had often shared a drink and a meal with, but they were so in love, so together, it made Ava want to weep.

'We heard about James.' And they were a nice couple, just up front, and she should be grateful that they faced it, that they didn't pretend that they didn't know. Except she was starting to cry—she was sitting in the middle of Pete's and starting to cry.

'Ava,' Mia put her arm on her shoulder but she pushed it off and stood.

'Leave me, please…' She didn't even pay for her wine, just stood up and walked out. She saw Mia's eyes close in regret for her handling of things, except they hadn't been insensitive, they were doing what everyone said you should: facing it, bringing it out in the open, talking about it.

She never wanted to hear those words again.

She walked home, thinking of the babies James would have with another. She had so often blended their features—amber-eyed babies with light brown hair, or green-eyed babies with their hair dark—but now she had to take herself out of the picture.

Her blouse was sticking to her again, and as she stepped into the air-conditioned lobby at Kirribilli she shivered as she waited for the lift. Tears were really starting to come and she didn't know how to stop them. She pressed the lift button again, relieved when the doors opened. As she stood inside, pressing the button for her floor, someone raced to catch it, and she was quietly relieved that it was only Finn.

And because it was Finn, of course he ignored her.

He was having surgery first thing tomorrow too, but unlike James he was spending his last night at home.

Ava glanced at the bottle he must have gone out to purchase, figured a sleeping pill would be the safer option, but it was none of her business.

Neither nodded.

Neither bothered pretending it was a good evening.

They just both wished the lift would start moving. She was holding on to her tears for dear life, but they kept slipping out and her breath was coming out in little shudders and she just wished the lift would move.

'Looks like we're walking.' Finn broke the tense silence after several of Ava's frantic attempts at pushing buttons.

'Looks like it,' Ava said through gritted teeth.

She pushed open the stairwell door, and didn't hold it open, which was maybe a bit mean with his crippled arm, but she was past caring and started climbing. She could hear Finn behind her, determined to keep up with her, probably to prove he wasn't in pain.

She wanted to start running.

She just wanted to be in her flat so the tears could fall more readily, but even if she wanted to run her legs seemed to be turning to lead. She gripped the hand rail, moved one foot in front of the other, could hear Finn catching up, and she couldn't move a step further. She was doubled up in pain, not bleeding this time as Finn came up behind her. The pain wasn't physical, but it paralysed her just the same.

'Leave me,' she sobbed as he walked past her and she sat on the stairs, grateful that if someone had to see her like this it was Finn, because he was perhaps the only man who would walk straight past, because no doubt he just wanted to get up to his flat too. It was a relief to hear his footsteps pass, to just sit with her face buried in her hands and to weep, to give in to the tears and just let them fall. Later she would try to summon the energy to move.

She didn't hear him come back down, as she was crying too hard to notice his about-turn. She just sort of felt him on the stairs beside her, but she was too far gone to stop.

She hadn't cried like this in years.

Oh, there had been nightly tears for a long time now, but she hadn't actually broken down, not since she'd had the second miscarriage.

She hadn't sobbed so hard she thought she might vomit, that she might never again be able to breathe, in ages, but she did it now, sat on the stairs with Finn beside her and shuddered her pain out, and it seemed to echo through the stairwell. Surely people would come soon and tell her to shut the hell up, but she was shutting up anyway. Somehow the sobs were slowing down.

'Do you want some?' She glanced over as he opened the bottle.

'I really wish you'd just kept walking.'

'Believe me, I tried.' He handed her the bottle and she took a sip. She hadn't had whisky in years, hadn't had a glass of wine in years either. She had just kept on giving up everything she liked in the hope of keeping a baby inside her, and never going back to them again—just giving up all the things that made her her. And she didn't like who she was any more.

She didn't like the nitpicking, low-carb, healthy version of herself.

And she cried some more, but not so violently now. Finn just sat there and let her, and she took another swig of his drink.

'I don't want to talk,' Ava said.

'Good,' Finn answered. 'Because neither do I.'

They sat, him in silence, Ava still catching her breath as the tears started to slow, her body shuddering with little hiccoughs as it slowly calmed. Then she remembered it was his drink and Ava handed the bottle back to him. 'Should you be…?' And then she stopped herself because it wasn't her business and he too wanted silence and she was surprisingly grateful that he was there, but he declined when she offered him his drink.

'I think you need it more than me.'

She didn't. She took the lid and put it back on. They sat a while longer, her tears slowing down, the hiccoughs silencing, and it had actually been better here than alone. Finally, she could think about moving those last steps to her door as she sat there, still catching her breath from her crying marathon.

'I think the chivalrous thing to do would be to put my arm around you,' said Finn, 'except I can hardly feel it.'

She turned and gave him a very watery smile and after a moment's pause he returned it.

She'd never really looked at him, never really understood what Evie saw in him. James was macho, but Finn could be a bastard at times, yet he'd always been quietly nice to her and he was being quietly nice to her now.

And Finn looked at Ava. He'd never really been able to work her out. He liked James a lot, he was a bloke's bloke, and they'd shared more than a few nights at Pete's. But Ava—she was a funny little thing. At times he'd heard their rows, but she was always so prim and guarded when they met in the corridor. Even when she'd had the miscarriage, she'd hardly said a word, just 'Call James,' but surely she wasn't so prim and guarded? He knew what she did for a job. 'Lucky guy,' he'd ribbed James at times when they'd shared a drink at Pete's. 'Married to a sex therapist.'

Except he knew now how stupid those words

had been. He'd had to see that Donald a couple of weeks ago, a requirement for the surgery he was having, and hadn't liked one bit the details that Donald had gone into. He had firmly decided he wouldn't be seeing him again.

His smile turned wry as both sat on the steps, staring at the other, and it was Finn who broke the strange silence. 'You know, we could really mess things up here,' Finn said, removing his gaze from her and looking at their surroundings. 'We could have drunken sex on the stairwell…'

And she actually found herself laughing.

'Except I'd hate myself even more in the morning,' Finn said.

'Hate yourself?' Ava frowned.

'Guilt.'

'I didn't know you possessed such a thing.'

'Neither did I. But it'd be there tomorrow—you know, when Evie tries to come and see me to wish me well for the operation.'

She doubted a man like Finn had ever felt guilty before, had ever felt so loyal to a woman before, and he looked at her for a very long moment and she looked back at him. And then he spoke. 'And I'd hazard a guess that the only person you want to have sex with is your husband…'

It was true, so very true.

He stood up; he'd done enough sentiment for one night.

'Here.' She handed him the bottle, but he shook his head.

'Better not. Better still that the lift isn't working and I'll have to climb up these stairs again if I change my mind.'

He headed back up towards his penthouse suite as she sat on the step. 'Hey, Ava?'

'The answer is no.' She turned and smiled as she hauled herself up to go home, except his face was serious.

'If I end up in a chair…if I…' He closed his

eyes. 'I don't want Evie and I coming in to see you for help, don't want to be sitting in your office being told… I don't want to do that to her.'

Ava went over to him. 'Let her in, Finn.'

She saw the conflict knit his face closed, knew then how badly he wanted Evie there and understood too why he was pushing her away.

'And I'd help you,' she said, and wondered how she would deal with such a complicated, private man, because there was something about Finn, something about his brilliance that was intimidating. But she knew that if it came to it, and if he let her, she would help him.

'I don't want all that for her.' He shook his head. 'I saw that Donald…'

'You'd see me,' she said firmly. 'And *I* would help you, I would help both of you,' Ava promised as he shook his head to decline. Sometimes a bit of humour *was* needed. 'On the condition that you promise not to make one of those awful jokes.'

'What one's that?' Finn asked.

'Well, I never thought I'd end up in here.' She put on a macho male voice.

'You'll need the biggest one!' Finn gruffed back.

'They all say that.' Ava laughed.

'I *would* help you,' Ava said, joking over now, and her voice was kind as she did what she never thought she would to this dark, moody man—gave him a cuddle. And he put his good arm around her and they stood and held each other for a moment.

'We'll go back to ignoring each other tomorrow,' Ava assured him.

'I'm back to ignoring you now,' Finn said, but as he let her go, as he turned to go, he paused. 'Ring him,' Finn said, because he knew how cold and lonely James must be feeling tonight.

'Ring her,' Ava said, except she knew Finn wasn't going to take her advice. Was she going to take his?

Ava had a shower and washed her hair. It would be dry and frizzy tomorrow because there was never any conditioner in this place. She pulled on her robe and went through to the lounge and looked out of the window to the hospital where tonight James lay. She scanned the windows and tried to work out which was his room, wondered if he was looking out now towards their home.

She should be with him, Ava realised.

They should be in bed right now, making love—because she loved him and she had to tell him, and it was pure need that drove her impulse to pick up the phone.

'James.'

'Ava.' he sounded in no mood to talk. 'They've just given me a sleeping tablet.'

'I love you.'

'Look.' He was very practical, had anticipated that she must be feeling as guilty as hell by the timing of everything. 'We'll talk about this another time. We're over, Ava. You don't have to—'

'I want you here.'

James frowned as he heard her carefully formed words. 'Have you been drinking?'

'Yes.'

'How much?'

She looked at the bottle. 'Not much, but I haven't had anything for ages.' And then she remembered. 'Oh, and I had some wine too…'

'You lush!' She could picture his smile.

'God, James, I wanted to come to that room and help you…'

'You really have been drinking!' He grinned, remembered the times in their marriage when they would share a bottle of wine, and she carried on talking, told him she loved him, and even if they weren't going to make it, it was nice to hear it tonight, to talk to her, to hear her voice.

She wandered as she spoke, walked into the

bedroom and then to the en suite, where there were towels all over the floor, and about four razors because there was no way a nurse was shaving him.

'Are you bald?'

She should have shaved him and she said what she was thinking.

'I should have shaved you.'

'Ava.'

'No, I should have…' And she told him how she would have.

'Hell, Ava.' His hand was under the sheets. 'I'm going to have to press the bell and get them to bring in another specimen jar soon.'

They were both laughing.

'My wife the sex therapist.'

CHAPTER FIVE

'WE NEED you over on the trolley.'

Ava stood outside with Veronica as James was transferred to the trolley that would take him to Theatre. The warmth from last night had gone and she wasn't so shallow as to try and rekindle it. This morning wasn't about them, it was about James. He had been gruff and impatient when Lily the nurse had come in to take his obs and was equally gruff with his responses as she checked off the theatre list. Not that she seemed to mind. Lily was a friend of theirs—or rather Lily's husband Luke was a friend of James's and she and Lily always said they must catch up—they'd been to Luke and Lily's wedding. It just made it all the more awkward, though, but apparently not for

Lily—she smiled over to where Veronica and Ava stood and Ava tried not to look at Lily's pregnancy bump. 'Just one of you can come down to Theatre with him.'

'I'll be fine,' James said.

'Don't be ridiculous,' Ava said, and Veronica said she might go for a wander, but, as she walked alongside him, she wondered if James actually wanted her there, if she was just making this harder than it had to be. James stared up at the ceiling as she walked alongside the trolley to Theatre and his responses were just as curt as the theatre nurse now checked off the list.

'Two crowns,' he said for perhaps the tenth time since last night. 'Front two,' he said again. And Ava could not help but remember the rugby accident when he'd been at uni where he had lost his two front teeth and broken his nose. A few days later his father, Edward, had died, and he'd had temporary crowns for the funeral…

There was so much of their history in each box the nurse ticked.

'No,' he snapped when she asked if he had any allergies, though he was, in fact, allergic to Play-Doh. Veronica had told her that he'd had came home from school when he was five, all covered in welts—not that the nurses needed to know that. Maybe it was good that she'd come up with him after all—she could just imagine Veronica chiming in, which wouldn't have been the best with James in this mood!

Still, all too soon he was all checked off to their satisfaction and was ready to be wheeled through, and it was time to say goodbye.

'Say goodbye, have a kiss,' the cheerful theatre nurse said. 'He'll be out soon. The operation usually takes about an hour, sometimes a bit more, but we'll page when he's in Recovery and about to head back to the ward.'

Ava leant over him and stared into those green eyes.

'Good luck.' How paltry those words sounded. She went to kiss him but he turned his face so all she got was the edge of his mouth and his cheek and then he closed his eyes and said nothing, and she wanted five minutes away from everyone, just five minutes of his time, but since he'd found that awful lump they'd had none.

That dreadful morning was burned into her brain.

'James?' She could hear her question that morning, knew in an instant what he'd found.

She'd sort of dragged him to the bed, all sensible and reassuring, with her heart hammering in her chest. She'd felt for the lump and, yes, there was one, and she'd been all practical and agreed that, yes, he should get it seen to, except James had snapped into action by then—had been off the bed and ringing a colleague, and from that moment on it had been round after round of tests and scans.

And because it was James it had all been rushed through. They didn't do biopsies for testicular cancer—instead, it was ultrasounds and blood tests and CTs and counselling. And then he'd had to go round and tell his mother and then his mother had told the rest of his family and of course there had been uncles and cousins and just too many people coming over at night.

And when they went, so too did James's smile.

He was back on the sofa—his choice now, and using her own excuses against her.

'I'm tired, Ava.' That was one of them. 'I need space.' The other.

So she stood for a moment, watching him being wheeled away behind the black plastic doors, and as she turned around to go she saw Evie standing next to Finn. She was trying to talk to Finn, but his face was as closed as James's, staring over her shoulder, and then

Finn's eyes met Ava's for a very brief moment and maybe last night had affected them both because she watched as he did turn to Evie.

As he let her kiss him.

'I'll always be there for you, Finn.'

And she wanted to step in.

Wanted to tell Evie just to kiss him.

Wanted to somehow explain that her saying she would always be there for him was what terrified Finn most.

But as she looked at the black plastic doors, she wanted to run to her husband, wanted to say the same words to him.

Except he'd assume he was being given the sympathy vote.

Even though Ava's heart and mind were consumed with James, she couldn't help but feel for Evie as Finn was wheeled off. She felt for Finn too and, based on their conversation last night, the best she could do for Finn was to go over as Evie stopped trying to be strong. She felt the other woman almost implode beneath her fingers as she put her hand on her shoulder.

'Come on,' Ava said. 'We'll go to my office.'

Evie held it together till they were there but once away from the sympathetic stares and curious eyes, she broke down. 'I'm sorry,' she sobbed. 'It's your *husband* that's having surgery and I'm not being much help at all.'

'It's fine,' Ava said, because she'd had her tears yesterday and could at times be terribly, terribly practical, and also because she did not want to think of the paltry last words she and James had exchanged, did not want to spend the next couple of hours going over what was happening in Theatre, because she could not stand to think of him being operated on now. As complicated as Evie and Finn's relationship was, right now their problems were easier for Ava to deal with than her own. 'This is the easy bit for James. It's going to be hell waiting for the results and then finding out what's going to happen in the way of treatment, but today's really quite straightforward. Finn's surgery is far more serious.'

'Still…' Evie attempted.

'Hey, I spend the next couple of hours in here, or back on the ward with Veronica.' She rolled her eyes. 'My mother-in-law.'

'Don't you get on?' Evie was dabbing her eyes now. For all her tears she was much calmer today than Ava had been last night. Evie was a tough thing really, Ava thought. Though she'd probably had to be, given the family she'd come from.

'Not really,' Ava admitted. 'I don't think I've fulfilled the role of James's wife very well in her eyes. By now I should be a stay-at-home mum and have given her at least two little Carmichaels.'

'Don't you want children?'

And Ava had her lists of answers for that one, as if printed out in her mind so she could reel off the one that suited best. *Not for ages* or *Maybe someday* or *Not you too!* Or, said with a wry laugh to her more feminist friends, *I'd have expected better from you.* But today she didn't have the list handy. Today she was aching inside, today she was touched too, that from the innocence of Evie's question she knew Finn really had never told anyone about that time. And maybe it was time to be honest.

'We'd have loved to have had children,' Ava said. 'It just didn't work out that way.'

'Ava!'

'Evie, please.' Ava put her hand up. 'Can we talk about you and Finn, because I can't break down today, I truly can't— I don't want to go in to see James all upset. I'm sure he's worried enough as it is without me breaking down on him.' Oh, God, how easily she could—she could kick the wall in this very minute because yet again another block had been put in their path to parenthood.

'What did Finn say when you said goodbye?' Ava asked instead as she filled a glass of water from the sink and drained it and then managed to turn around and play calm.

'He said, "Bye, princess."' Evie gave a very watery smile. 'He calls me that, sometimes nastily…' Ava could imagine. Evie's father had donated so much to the hospital and everyone had once assumed that Evie had had some sort of free pass in the hospital so it was a bit of a nickname around the place and she could well imagine Finn using that barb.

'But he didn't say it nastily today. I know Finn can be a complete bastard…'

And had Ava not sat on the stairs and spoken with him last night, she might have inwardly agreed, except… 'There's a lot more to Finn than that,' Ava said. 'And this operation is just huge. I can't imagine what he's going through.'

'We're not going to know the outcome for

ages,' Evie said. 'He's asked me not to visit. How am I supposed to stay away?'

'I don't know,' Ava said. 'Maybe…' Despite her best efforts she couldn't stop thinking about James, couldn't stop comparing the two men, which was ridiculous as they were completely different. 'Maybe just give him space,' she advised, but her heart wasn't in it because she could not stand that now for James and herself—and maybe sometimes it was better to admit the truth.

'I don't know, Evie. I don't know what to suggest. I think you just have to get through this bit for now.'

It was terribly hard to take her own advice, though.

'How much longer?' Veronica was pacing when Ava came down.

'It shouldn't be much longer now,' Ava said.

'And then the real wait begins.' Which it did,

because they'd have to wait to find out for sure what they were dealing with.

'I know it's hard.'

'No, Ava, you don't,' Veronica said. 'He's my son.'

Ava tried not to take it personally but, hell, it felt personal and terribly so, as if unless she was a mother she didn't really know love, and of course Veronica hadn't meant that, but it stung, that was all.

'He's all I've got,' Veronica said, and it took all Ava's might to bite her tongue, to not point out that at least she'd had a child. There was a froth of anger inside her, like the type that washed up on the beach after a filthy storm, and Ava hated what the last days had done, not just to James but also to her.

'I'm just going up to Theatre to get him.' Lily popped her head around the door. 'I shouldn't be long.'

She wasn't. About ten minutes later Ava

and Veronica stood outside in the hall again as James was transferred back to his bed, and then they waited outside while Lily did his obs and made him comfortable. Finally they were allowed in.

'Hey.' She bent her head and he was too groggy to turn his face away this time. She could smell the fumes of the anesthetic and she was so pleased to see him back. 'How do you feel?'

'Tired,' James said, and promptly went back to sleep.

And Veronica had been right, because now the real wait started, and time seemed to be moving terribly slowly. When his next set of obs were done half an hour later, Veronica gave in to a headache and said that she would go but would be popping over to the apartment that evening. 'Do you need me to bring anything?'

'We're fine,' Ava said. 'I'll text you when we get home.'

And there were more obs and he woke up and was sick once, and he got annoyed with her and told her to go. Then he woke up again and was more like James.

'You might as well go.' James said it a lot more nicely this time. 'I'll be a few hours yet.'

'I'm not going anywhere,' Ava said. 'Well, I might go and get a drink and I'll text people, let them know you're okay.'

'Get some lunch,' James suggested.

She did, except she didn't have it in the canteen. Instead, Ava bought a salad sandwich and a bottle of water and sat outside in the sun. It was nice to be outside, Ava realised. She didn't do this nearly enough. Most of her lunches she took in her office.

She looked out at the water. They hadn't been on the water in ages. They used to get the ferry, just hop off wherever and get breakfast when James had a weekend off. She would love to do it this weekend, but of course he wouldn't be able to, but maybe next, Ava decided, or maybe the weekend before he went back to work.

If they weren't over by then.

She felt like a fighter pilot, scrambling for a plan when already it was too late, but she sat in the sun, making lists in her mind of all the things they would do. They'd play Scrabble, and talk, or she'd just lie on the bed beside him and read. And, please, God, that the results weren't too bad, because there were so many things James had to do and so many things she wanted to do with him, and it was simply too hard to think like that today, so she stood and binned her half-eaten sandwich and then headed back to the ward.

When she returned the door was closed and as Ava walked in, Lily called from behind a drawn curtain and asked Ava to wait outside as she was just checking James's wound. That just seemed stupid to Ava—she'd seen it all before!—but she turned around obediently and went out to the corridor.

'Won't be long.' Lily popped out but closed the door behind her, and as she headed off to the supplies trolley she gave Ava a smile. Perhaps a bit rudely Ava didn't return it. Instead, she stood bristling in the corridor as Lily returned, holding a couple of medical packs.

She was being petty, Ava knew that. She and Lily shared a mutual love of horses and at Christmas dos and the like they sort of gravitated towards each other. Today she had been nothing but nice but Ava could not return her smile.

'Blake's going to come down and see him,' Lily said.

'Why?' Ava snapped, because Blake was an oncologist like James and this operation was being dealt with by the surgical team.

'He just wants to check in on him,' Lily explained.

'And then we can go home?' Ava checked, because she wanted so badly to be home with him, alone with him. Maybe when they got there she could ring Veronica and say that James was asleep and not to worry about coming over. But instead of answering her question, Lily gave that noncommittal smile that nurses did so well and disappeared back into the room, leaving Ava still standing in the corridor, tears stinging in her eyes.

She couldn't help it. She was jealous of Lily—her pregnancy, her happy marriage and healthy husband. She'd dealt with not being able to have a baby of her own, but today everything felt so raw that she was even jealous that it was Lily in with her husband now. So jealous of Lily, who would no doubt trot and canter her way through a textbook pregnancy.

Oh, God, what was wrong with her? Why was she thinking such horrible things?

Ava didn't know how she felt.

She hardly managed a smile when Blake appeared.

'I'm just going to take a look at him, Ava.' And after a few moments she was called into the room and she still didn't know how she felt as she stood there.

'The surgeons say that everything went really well today,' Blake said. 'However, he's still got some considerable pain and is nauseous, so we're going to keep him in overnight.' Blake confirmed what she'd guessed was happening—knew the little powwow he and Lily had had behind that closed door. 'He should be fine to go home tomorrow morning.'

'Thanks, Blake.' James shook his hand from his bed and then Blake left the room.

'I'll come back with your injection shortly,' Lily said, and left them alone.

'You didn't say you were in a lot of pain.'

'I didn't want to moan,' James replied. 'You might as well go home.'

'I can stay.'

'There's no point,' James said. 'I'll just be sleeping once I get the needle. When you get home can you ring Mum and tell her that they're keeping me in?'

'You know she'll just want to visit,' Ava said.

'Of course she will,' James said. 'I'm her son.'

'Here's your injection, James.' Lily came back in carrying a little kidney dish and she was going to swoosh that curtain any second, Ava knew it, and ask her to step outside, but it was James who spoke next.

'I'll see you, then, Ava.' And she knew that she was being dismissed. Ava didn't bother with the kiss goodbye for appearances' sake. Sure, he probably was in pain, but at the bottom of her heart Ava knew, and she knew that Lily knew, that James had told her and Blake that he'd prefer hospital to home.

* * *

She rang Veronica and told her of the development and, of course, Veronica informed her that she was heading back soon. 'I might take him in some dinner.'

Ava didn't bother with dinner—she was, in fact, exhausted.

She had a shower and climbed into bed, weary with fatigue, but her brain was going at a hundred miles an hour, and when her phone bleeped a text she jumped up, wondering if it was the hospital, hoping it was James, and then felt a little guilty when she saw that it was Evie, because she'd completely forgotten about Finn.

Finn out of Theatre and Recovery and now on ICU. Way too early to say how it went but thankfully operation over.

It was a group text, Ava knew that. She'd sent one of her own to their family and friends when James had been returned to the ward. As nice as it was that people were thinking of them, the multitude of replies and questions had been somewhat overwhelming, so Ava did Evie a favour and didn't reply.

Just closed her eyes, relieved for Finn, scared for Finn.

Relieved for James, scared for James.

Scared for herself too.

CHAPTER SIX

JAMES texted in the morning and asked if she could bring up a coffee when she picked him up, so she stopped at the kiosk and waited while it was being made and noticed that her hand was shaking as she handed over the money.

She was nervous about seeing him and she didn't want to be.

'Oh, hi, Tom.' She turned as someone came up beside her, and because Tom was blind Ava introduced herself. 'It's Ava.'

'Ava!' Tom smiled. 'I've just come over to have coffee with Hayley—and to bring Sasha to see her mum. Hayley's on call all weekend.'

She glanced over to where Hayley, who was a surgeon, sat engrossed in her baby.

'How are you?' Tom asked.

'Good.' Ava said, because Tom must be the only person who didn't know, but he worked over at the university, and she simply didn't have the energy to talk about it today, and they seemed to be taking for ever to froth the coffee. *Oh, please,* Ava thought, *just hurry up.*

'And James?' Tom added, because he couldn't see the desperation in her eyes.

'Yeah, he's not bad,' Ava said, and did her best to keep her voice light and smiled as the cashier handed her her change, except she dropped all the coins on the floor. 'Sorry.'

She scrabbled to the floor and saw Tom's dog, Baxter, and wanted to weep onto him as she picked up her change. Instead, when she'd collected the coins she stayed kneeling for a moment and stroked his beautiful head.

'Ava.' Tom's voice came from a long way off. 'You can't pat Baxter.'

'Of course. Sorry.' She pulled her hand away and stood.

'While he's got his harness on, he's not to be patted,' Tom explained, and he was right, of course. Baxter was working, she'd simply forgotten, and Tom was only being nice, only saying what he must have to about a hundred times a day, yet it felt like a snub. Of course it wasn't a snub, but she was so prickly and raw that everything hurt a little more.

'I'll bring your coffees over, Tom,' the cashier said when she took his order, and Ava said goodbye as he headed back to his family. A little later as she took her coffee she saw Hayley speaking with Tom, saw Tom wince, knew that now Hayley was telling him.

Blake was there with James when she got up to the ward and so too was Lily. She looked tired today, but she was all smiles when Ava came in as Blake finished off giving his discharge instructions. Ava stood there as Lily hauled over a wheelchair and Ava wondered what on earth she was doing working. Her husband was a consultant after all…

And then she stopped herself, because so was hers and she'd worked, she believed in women working. She was just being horrible, jealous and vile and bitter, and— She didn't know how she felt.

'And Lily has given you all the after-care instructions.' Blake finished up as Ava struggled to concentrate on what was being said.

'I've got everything,' James broke in. 'And I'm not being wheeled down.'

'No choice.' Lily beamed. 'It's a long way to the foyer.'

As James took a reluctant seat Ava handed him his coffee.

'Thanks,' he said.

'Thanks, Blake,' Ava said. It felt strange to be speaking with him in this way—normally she only saw Blake at social events, sometimes when he came with his wife, Joan, to the apartment for dinner. 'I guess we now just have to wait till we get the results.'

'Yes.' James was clearly itching to get out of the hospital. 'Give me a ring as soon as you get *my* results.'

'Of course,' Blake said, and as his eyes briefly met Ava's, she felt a dull flush spread up her cheeks and it refused to go. There were tears at the back of her eyes too as the porter wheeled James down, Lily walking alongside. That blasted flush stayed on her cheeks as she went and got the car, and as she realised she'd forgotten her swipe card to get out of the staff car park the tears started trickling.

But she'd got into the car park, she told herself, so it had to be here, and she rummaged through her bag to look for it. She settled for a tissue instead and wept into it for a moment.

'Stop it, Ava.' She said it about four times. She should have done this at home, last night. 'Not here.'

And she dragged in a breath and rubbed some powder on her face and found her stupid swipe card and drove to where James was waiting with Lily, who was chatting easily with him.

And she knew how she felt then.

Knew the word she'd been searching for these past days.

Excluded.

Excluded from everything.

'I can manage.' He refused her help, just climbed into the passenger side, and he would have driven himself home if he'd been allowed to, Ava realised.

'Thanks.' She tried to smile at Lily, except her mouth wouldn't move.

'You're welcome.' Lily patted her arm. 'We'll catch up soon, Ava.'

They hardly said a word during the short drive home, and there was Veronica waiting at the door as he limped out of the lift.

Excluded.

That was how she felt as Veronica made James's lunch and suggested Ava go to the store and get some more ice for James's ice packs.

And he was the last mummy's boy on earth, but he did love his mum enough to *let* her look after him.

He slept for most of the afternoon then got up and had some dinner, cooked by Veronica, then stood up and declared he was going back to bed.

'Thanks.' He gave Veronica a kiss. 'Go home, Mum.'

'You're sure?'

'I just want to go to bed. Thanks for everything.'

Ava saw her out and then headed back to the lounge but James had already gone to the bedroom and was pulling back the sheets.

'Did you need anything?'

'I just want to go to sleep.'

'Sure,' Ava said. 'I'll bring you in a fresh ice-pack when I come to bed.' She went to head out, didn't want his words to catch her before she closed the door, but it was as if James had been waiting for them.

'Ava. I really appreciate you giving up *your* bed for a couple of nights.'

'James, please.' Ava swallowed. 'Let me come to bed.'

'You can do what you want, but if you get into this bed I swear I'll get straight out and check into a hotel.'

'James, I don't want you in a hotel.' She didn't and she didn't want something else too. 'I don't want a divorce. Can you just listen?'

'No, you listen!' he broke in. 'It was *your* miscarriages, *your* babies, *your* grief, you made it that way—well, it's *my* cancer. And do you know what I don't need now? I don't need to be one of your clients in this, I don't want you telling me that you can't feel the difference in my balls, or your patronising understanding when I'm so scared or drugged up that I can't get it up. Neither do I want sympathy sex, or any of it. The same way I didn't want you in there when I was getting my dressing changed. You didn't want any of it when I was well…'

She couldn't even cry.

'And—' he hadn't finished yet '—I heard you saying to Mum that you had taken a week off. Well, you can untake it, because I won't be able to rest or relax with you in the flat. What was it you used to say when I tried to give you a cuddle or, heaven forbid, a kiss? What was it you used to say when I tried to talk? Oh, I remember: "I need space." In your own words, Ava!'

CHAPTER SEVEN

JAMES was closed.

There might as well have been a sign around his neck—'Not back in five minutes, not open again soon.'

He was completely closed.

He'd done a similar thing when his dad had died, a week after his teeth had been knocked out. He'd just shut her off, only for a couple of days, but by the funeral, when all the bruises had looked brown and yellow, they had been together again, close again, making love again. Not that he'd ever really broken down about his dad—not once in their relationship had James cried, not even when she'd lost the babies. He just didn't do tears, and he wasn't doing them now—if anything, as the weekend passed, more and more he seemed quietly cheered.

He rang friends for chats, he sat on the computer for an hour on Sunday and bought about fifty books for his ereader and then, before he went back to bed, he ordered a pizza.

And, no, Ava noted, he didn't offer her a slice, but, then, why would he when she'd always refused before?

It was incredibly uncomfortable on the sofa and she'd forgotten to put her clothes out the night before, but he didn't wake up as she rummaged through her wardrobe early on Monday morning, neither did he wake up when she showered and did her hair.

Or maybe he was pretending to be asleep.

And then she felt the stab of regret as she qualified it—maybe he was pretending to be asleep, just as she had.

'What are you doing back?' he asked later that day, when she popped back on her lunch break.

He was sitting in bed on the phone, but hung up when she came in.

'I just thought I'd check how you were.'

'I'm fine.' He had a computer game on, and if anything seemed to be treating it as a holiday. He hadn't shaved since they'd found the lump, and he was looking like he did whenever they had time off, sort of scruffy and rumpled and actually, impossibly perhaps, happy.

Unlike Ava.

'And there was some news on Finn I thought you might want to hear.'

'Yeah, I heard.' He nodded to the phone on the bed beside him. 'They didn't cut my ears off, Ava.'

And it was so James that if she'd paused for a moment, she might even have laughed, except there was nothing to laugh about today. It wasn't good news about Finn and she ached to speak with James about it. There was shrapnel they hadn't been able to reach and the attempts at removal had made things worse. Right now he was ventilated and in spinal shock. However, she pressed on with a conversation James didn't want.

'It doesn't look good for Finn,' she offered, but James just shrugged and went back to his game.

'Early days,' he said.

'I'll stop and get something nice for dinner,' Ava attempted, 'maybe take-away?'

'If you want,' James said, 'but not for me. I've got a freezer full of stuff from Mum.' And to prove his point he swung his legs out of bed and, much more easily now, walked over to the fridge and grabbed some herbed chicken and stir-fried rice, which was his favourite. Veronica had made loads, of course, and he popped his individual serving, which would feed a horse, into the microwave.

Yet for all his unhealthy eating he looked, and

she really shouldn't be noticing such things, fantastic.

He had some bruising down his thigh and had a support on, but over that was new underwear, really sexy, modern underwear—from his shopping trips in Brisbane, Ava reminded herself.

Except she wasn't jealous at the moment, and she wasn't even upset. She was just looking at him, not at his eyes but at his chest and then down to his thigh and that bruise and then up to his flat stomach. Then she met his gaze and he snapped his eyes away, and she didn't know the hows and whys but if it had been another day, another time, they'd have already been on the floor, and she knew he knew it. He sort of grimaced a little bit and moved his support as he walked across the kitchen and his muscles were rippling as he reached into the fridge and pulled out a milk carton, and as if to defy her, because it was one of the few things she really *was* closed-minded on, he drank straight from the carton, then burped and drank again. When the microwave pinged he took his chicken and milk back to the bedroom with him and closed the door.

Maybe it was only she who had wanted to make love, then, Ava conceded.

Maybe he *was* happy it was over.

She stood in the kitchen, and faced the impossible truth.

Maybe he was simply relieved.

She went to walk out, opened the front door and stood a moment, and then closed it, because they had to talk, because, no, he couldn't be happy, he couldn't be relieved. She knew them better than that, knew how good they were, how good they had been. She could not live this a single moment longer so she drew in a breath, tried to gather the strength to just walk in the bedroom and force him to listen, except she could hear the blips as, assuming she'd gone out, he dialled a number on the phone and then came his voice.

'Yeah, sorry, Steph… It's okay, she's gone back to work. Nearly got caught there! Now, where were we?'

CHAPTER EIGHT

'I'M SORRY about this, Donald.'

'It's not a problem,' Donald said as Ava sat on a chair on the other side of his desk, pulling tissues from his box. 'Ginny has cancelled your clients for the afternoon.'

'Thanks.'

His office was so different from hers, his style, his stance the complete opposite of hers, yet *his* patients adored him. His brusque, direct approach was one that appealed to some, though Ava wasn't particularly grateful for it now, not grateful that he tutted and tsked as she poured out a little more of what was going on. 'You shouldn't have come in this week,' Donald said. 'You've got far too much going on to be sensible at work.'

'I know that,' Ava shrilled. 'But James doesn't want me at home. What am I supposed to do, spend the day walking on the beach?'

'You could ask him,' Blake said. 'Ask him if he's seeing someone else.'

'I could,' Ava said. 'And whether you believe me or not, if he didn't have this diagnosis hanging over him I would.' She held her breath at the impossibility of it all. 'That's a whole lot of arguing to cram in between now and next week when he gets his results. Can I forgive him?' She didn't know. Sometimes she thought she could, sometimes she knew she never could. They needed time, time to thrash things out, but time was the commodity they'd frittered away so foolishly and now suddenly it was running out.

'Maybe check yourself into some hotel like he's threatening to.' Donald smiled. 'Spend the day in bed, getting room service.'

Ava was surprised to find herself smiling back. 'That's worryingly tempting.'

'Do it, then.' Donald shrugged.

'That's no answer.'

'Well, you're probably not getting much rest on that sofa.' He took a breath. 'Ava, you know James will be feeling scared, he'll also be angry…'

'He's not, though.'

'Ava?'

And she closed her eyes and thought about it, because Donald was right, James must be feeling those things, but then Donald pushed things too far. 'And he'll be feeling protective of you.'

'Of me?' Maybe Donald was from another planet after all.

'Of course he is. Even if your relationship was perfect at the moment, he'd still be behaving like this to some extent—he knows what's coming up better than anyone, maybe he doesn't want to put you through it too. Especially—'

'That's ridiculous—'

'Especially,' Donald spoke over her, 'if he thought the marriage was over anyway.'

'So what do I do?'

'What the man said,' Donald said. 'Give him some space. Give yourself some space too. Go home tonight with a take-away for one, and a movie and a pile of work. Let him get his own dinner, he's clearly capable. Buy a carton of milk and write your own name on it.

'But for now I'd suggest you go into that scruffy office of yours, take the phone off the hook, pull down the blinds and have a sleep.'

So she did.

She could hear the noises from the overhead loudspeaker and the murmur of Ginny on the phone, and for the first time since cancer had invaded, for the first time in a very long time, she slept.

And it helped.

And, to Donald's credit, his other suggestions actually helped too.

She shouted hi when she came in from work late, after seven, having stopped at her take-away, and she sat on the couch and ate noodles *with* chopsticks—from the box. James had always found that a bit pretentious. What the hell was the point when you had a drawer of forks and spoons? he would say. Well, James was in his room, so she used her chopsticks but ended up getting a spoon for the sauce at the bottom. She put on a movie, a movie that didn't involve guns, or worlds ending, or murder investigations, so there was no way it was a ploy to get him on the couch, and when he padded out a little bit later, she did hear a small laugh as he opened the fridge and must have seen 'Ava's milk'.

There was a pause.

Just a pause, and for that, after the days she'd had, she was terribly grateful.

CHAPTER NINE

JAMES knew the time lab results came in during the evening.

He knew too that things were being rushed through.

And though he'd told Ava and everyone else not to expect results till the middle of next week, on the Thursday evening after his surgery, just in case, he tried to log in and pull up his file, but Blake had locked him out and the lock remained.

He waited half an hour and then caved in, texted Blake to see if there was any news.

Out with Joan for wedding anniversary—will let you know as soon as I can.

He didn't say no. And James knew then that the next day he would know his results, that decisions would be made for the journey he was about to begin.

'Hi!' Ava walked in as he stood looking out of the window and as he turned to say hi, Ava smiled, but she was giving him the space he'd insisted on because she went straight through to the kitchen and poured herself a drink of water.

How could he put her through all this? James wondered.

He knew what lay ahead—knew as well as anyone who hadn't been through it all what lay ahead.

And for what?

James knew the statistics better than anyone, knew the odds were in his favour, that Donald was right, a future probably awaited him, but what if not?

He'd seen what losing the babies had done to Ava; he'd seen his vibrant, happy wife slowly go downhill to the point where their marriage was over.

A marriage that had, for a very long time, been such a good one.

And instead of staring out of the window, or slumping on to the couch or going back to his bedroom, when Ava went to the kitchen this time he followed her through.

'How was work?'

'Slow!' Ava said, opening the fridge, but there was nothing she fancied and she didn't want another take-away. 'Two patients cancelled. I'd have come home earlier except I went for a coffee with Evie.' She saw his vague frown as she turned round. 'We've sort of become friends.' And it just sort of underscored how little they spoke, so she asked after him. 'How are you doing?'

'I'm bored,' James said, which wasn't strictly true. His mind had never been so restless, but he wanted distraction very badly. 'I can't stand another week of this. I think I'm going to go back to work next week.'

'You haven't even been out of the flat,' Ava pointed out. 'You could go for a walk.' She said. 'Or we could, it's a nice—'

'I have been going for walks.' James said, and he sort of, almost, smiled. 'There was no choice, given there wasn't any milk.'

'There is milk…' Ava started, and then she sort of almost smiled too. 'If you want to get out a bit further than the corner shop, I could drive you to the beach.' She knew he'd say no, knew he'd just shake his head and head back to the bedroom that was his this week, except he didn't give the answer she was expecting. Instead, he nodded and walked out of the kitchen. 'I'll just get changed.'

She knew that James hated being driven so Ava was a little bit surprised, as they approached their local beach, when James suggested they drive on a bit further.

'How about the other beach?' James suggested. 'We haven't been there for a while.'

It had been their regular beach many years ago. James had been renting a large house along with some fellow students just a few hundred metres or so from the beach when she had first met him and as they drove past the house she saw James crane his neck for a glimpse of the house he had once lived in and the one she had also moved into.

'It still looks like a bombsite,' James said. It really was a renovator's delight, or maybe the whole thing would be better pulled down because from the front gate to the chimney work needed to be done, but they had known so many good times there. 'Its probably still being rented out to students.'

Ava parked the car as close as they could get to the beach and headed down the once familiar route. The sun was low on the water and the beach busy, with joggers and teenagers and couples like them, or people walking alone, just taking time to indulge, and the silence wasn't awkward, more pensive. It was James that broke it.

'Thanks for this. I think I was getting cabin fever.'

'It's nice to get out,' Ava agreed, because it really was. 'We used to go walking in the evenings a lot.' She gave him a nudge. 'Before you got all important.'

She was talking about his promotion a couple of years ago and instead of snapping back a smart retort as to how home hadn't actually been a bundle of laughs to race back to, James was silent for a moment as he walked on and thought about what she had said, because it was all so much more complicated than that. Feelings and events were so intricately intertwined that it was almost impossible to separate them, but on a night like tonight—when tomorrow everything changed—James did.

'Sorry about that.' She glanced over at his unexpected apology. 'I don't like rushing people,' James continued. 'I tried to put the difficult patients towards the end of the day, so I wasn't putting everyone else behind. You try and juggle it, to get the balance right.' He'd never really tried to explain it before. 'Like last week, when I found the lump, Blake moved his whole morning. And when my results come back I won't want just a ten-minute consultation.' Then he gave a wry laugh. 'Well, I might.'

He wanted a ten-minute incredulous apology from Blake actually, for Blake to tell him that they'd got it all completely wrong, that pathology had found nothing, nothing at all, and the blood tests were a complete mix-up, and Ava even smiled when he told her.

'I just hate pushing people through. I know I can't always take the time I'd like to, but seeing them later in the day…' He gave an uncomfortable shrug. 'It cost us, though, didn't it?'

'It wasn't just that,' Ava said, because they could have worked around that had things been better between them, then she saw him grimace. 'Are you okay?'

'Walking on the sand is harder than I thought,' James said, and he looked on ahead to a place that had once been theirs, where a much younger James and Ava had found out just how much they liked each other one night after a student party. But it was a place that seemed just a little bit too far away to get to this evening and as they turned and walked back towards the car, Ava wondered if James even remembered.

'Are you looking forward to the summer break?' James had asked.

They had wandered away from the party, the excuse being that it was too noisy to talk. Exams had finished and the summer had stretched ahead. Ava had lied when she'd answered him—after all, she couldn't really admit that she couldn't stand the thought of nearly three months of not seeing him. She'd had a crush on him for ages, they had spoken a couple of times, but now, just when they were really talking, just when it seemed things were starting to move on, she wouldn't see him for ages.

But of course she hadn't told him that. Instead she'd said that, yes, she was looking forward to it.

Then he'd asked, 'What plans have you got?'

'Well, it's my birthday in January and Mum and Dad have offered to get me a flight up to Queensland to go and visit my cousin.'

'A return flight, I hope?'

'I should check that, actually.' Ava had smiled as they'd sat down. 'I wouldn't put it past them.'

And she halted, because she really didn't want to talk about her parents, about how really every holiday for as long as she could remember she had been sent away, either to an auntie's or grandparent's, and now that she was older, the supposed gift was just another way to ensure she didn't get in her parents' way.

'I think I'll just ask them for the money instead. I'm going to be looking for a flat…' She really didn't fancy flat-sharing, but living at home wasn't working, and on her waitressing wage it was all she could afford.

'What about you?' Ava asked. 'Are you looking forward to it?'

'That depends,' James said, 'on whether or not I've got your phone number.'

Her breath seemed to burn in her lungs as he voiced what she had been thinking and her face was on fire as he moved towards her. And at eighteen, close to nineteen, she had her first kiss. Not that he knew it was her first, she hoped, and it certainly wasn't his, because James's mouth knew exactly what to do.

He stroked her lips with his and she felt his hand steady her head as he increased the pressure, as she tried to work out how to breathe with the man she had been thinking so much about finally close, and he simply didn't let her be clumsy or awkward, he just kissed her nervous lips till they gave in to the bliss, and just as her mouth accustomed to another on hers there was the shock of her first taste of tongue and another layer of bliss was exposed to her by him.

She struggled to contain it, to not simply melt beneath him as his lips pressed her down towards the sand. She was about to halt him, to stop him, except her mind asked her why, when it felt so nice with him over her.

His lips dragged from her mouth, to her cheeks, to her ear, and the feel of his hot breath there should surely not be so nice, or was it the words that had her unfurl?

'Don't go to Queensland,' James breathed. 'Spend the summer here.'

She could spend for ever here in his arms

being kissed. Then there was a bombardment of new sensations, his hand moving up from her waist, warm fingers sliding up beneath her T-shirt, and she knew she should halt him, that perhaps she was giving him the wrong idea about where this was leading.

She could feel the solid press of him against her sand-dusted thigh, and still, dangerously, she kissed him back, and as his hand found her breast she wanted it to stay there. James knew that, for she moaned into his mouth and then she pulled back from him, looked up at him, and he felt her sudden tension—her hands on his shoulders and a flash of uncertainty in her eyes—and James removed his hand and went back to simply kissing her.

All he'd done that night was kiss her. He'd spent the entire summer gradually taking each barrier down, dismantling each insecurity, taking things slowly, acting patiently as she drove him wild.

And he wondered if she even remembered.

'It doesn't look good for Finn,' James said as they headed back to the car, and they spoke for a bit about Finn, about how hard it was on Evie.

'She's still working,' Ava said. 'But any minute she's not she's either with him on ICU or asleep on the on-call room there.'

'Finn wouldn't want that,' James said.

'Well, while Finn's got a tube down his throat, he doesn't exactly have much say in things.'

And James wouldn't want that either, and he tried not to think of a time when it might be Ava catching some shut-eye in a camp bed by his side. Ava spoon-feeding him, Ava running herself ragged through the 'Till death us do part' bit. He was being ridiculous, he tried to tell himself for the hundredth time this evening because, yes, the statistics were good.

But the glass was resolutely stuck on half-empty—he simply couldn't get it to half-full.

They got back to the car and once there he

looked up at the house he had once lived in, looked at the room that had once been his, had been theirs, but it ached to remember that time, so he climbed into the car and they drove the length of the beach that they had used to come to so often. He didn't want it to be tomorrow, didn't want to get his results, even though he was desperate to hear them. He knew too much about what lay ahead, knew how hard it would be not just on him but also on them. All that he would put Ava through, and for what?

He looked over at Ava. Her face was pale from the strain of the last few days but, then again, it had been pale the day he'd come home from Brisbane. The strain of the last two years was taking its toll—he'd promised to make her happy and clearly hadn't been doing a very good job.

'Do you want to get something to eat?' James suggested. 'Maybe go to Pete's?'

'Sure,' Ava said, a little taken back at his suggestion. 'I hope I'm not banned.'

'Banned?'

And she told him, well, not all of it, but about how she'd been upset and had dashed off without paying for her wine.

'They'll have your photo up at the bar.' James smiled, but it was a pale one—he'd been trying to get her to go to Pete's for the last two years, but now that he had cancer his wish was her command. Suddenly everybody was treating him just a little bit differently—as they walked into the bar they ran into Lexi and Sam, casual friends from the hospital, but the conversation was forcibly jovial and he wanted things the way they had been before.

'That was awkward,' James said as he steered Ava to their regular spot by the window.

'Lexi has got a lot on her mind,' Ava said. 'She's probably really worried about Evie.' Lexi was one of Evie's sisters and even if they hadn't been so friendly then, Ava recalled when their younger sister, Bella, had had a lung transplant and how neither she nor James had known how to broach it in conversation. It was hard being in the medical profession at times like this, when you knew perhaps more than a friend should.

'Remember how awkward it was when Bella had her surgery? We didn't know what to say to Lexi then.'

'I guess.' James shrugged as he looked through the menu 'I might get pizza,' James said, only it wasn't to annoy her this time. It was what they used to share when they had first moved here, a family-sized mozzarella, and he'd have far more than half of it. 'And a beer,' he added, because no matter what these results were tomorrow, he was going on a health kick. Good news or bad, he was going to take a lot better care of himself from now on, he just needed this one last night.

'I'm going to have a steak.' Ava was suddenly hungry.

'You need to add a glass of wine to the bill.' James smiled as the waiter came over and he relayed their orders, adding 'medium-rare' to her steak and salad when the waiter asked what her side order was, because he knew how she liked things. 'She has a tendency to run off without paying.'

And as it turned out, the waiter did remember her, and he laughed as he told her that the other couple had picked up her bill.

It was actually a really nice evening. Ava couldn't quite work out James's mood, but they chatted a lot about old times and they certainly weren't maudlin. Well, maybe a little bit, because they were at their old table and by mistake, about half an hour into their time there, the waiter brought over a bottle of champagne they hadn't ordered.

'Sorry!' He smiled when James said with a

slightly wry note that they weren't celebrating. 'Wrong table.'

And they sat for a moment and neither said a word to each other. In fact, both looked away, but both surely remembered.

'I can't drink!'

They'd been almost deranged with excitement at the prospect of being parents, their hair still wet from the showers because as soon as she'd told him they'd started kissing and then ended up making love, and afterwards they'd decided to go out to Pete's to celebrate.

'You can have one glass.'

'No.' She'd been adamant, and so too had he, because he'd gone ahead and ordered a bottle and they'd sat holding hands and just grinning at their secret.

'When can we tell people?' James had asked.

'Twelve weeks,' Ava had said.

'That's ages,' James had moaned. 'Then again…' he'd rolled his eyes '…my mum is going to go crazy, you do know that? She's been waiting years for this.'

James would have had children straight away as soon as they were married had Ava wanted to. He adored kids, was a favourite with the children in his extended family. He couldn't wait for a family of his own, but Ava had really wanted to be established in her career first. Sexual dysfunction had never been her intended specialty—in fact, she had intended to be a GP—but somehow she had drifted towards that area, and it had only been when she'd got to thirty that she'd felt ready to make that commitment, but once ready she'd embraced it wholeheartedly.

The waiter popped the champagne and poured it.

'To twins.' James grinned.

'Please, no!' Ava said, and she did have a tiny taste as they clinked their glasses and said 'Cheers'.

It had been their last perfect night, really, and the last time she'd tasted champagne.

By the next morning she hadn't been pregnant any more.

James suggested they leave the car where it was parked outside Pete's and instead walk the short distance home. She wished he'd at least take her hand, longed for the days when he'd kissed her against a wall or all the way up in the lift were long gone now.

She wanted them back, so badly she wanted them back.

When they got home James put on a movie, not a crime show for once, and neither was it one Ava would have chosen. In fact, it was science fiction, of all things, with subtitles. It was a movie she'd didn't even know that they had.

'I've seen this before, I think.'

'I found it at the second-hand market,' James said, and he sat on the sofa beside her, just not close enough to touch.

She was sure she had seen it, or maybe not. It was the maddest film, but there was a certain sense of déjà vu to it, or at least there was for a little while, but halfway through she was lost.

'No.' Ava shook her head. 'I haven't seen this.' And then she frowned because she'd been quite sure she had.

She never had found a flat before the start of her first semester. She had arrived one night at the house, in tears after her parents had had a blistering row. James had been on his way out with his housemates, but had waved them off and they had stayed behind and gone where they'd always gone—to his room. And though they had done an awful lot of things, they hadn't quite done that.

'I'm sorry about this.'

'Sorry about what?' James had asked. They'd been lying on the bed just talking and kissing, they'd given up trying to make sense of her parents, of trying to work out if her mother actually was leaving her father this time.

'You were going out.'

'Now I'm staying in.' His hand crept up her leg and she didn't wriggle away. Instead her hands found him and more and more she moved him closer to where he stroked her with his fingers, and they almost had a few times before, and he wasn't sure he could play that game again, except he wasn't stroking her now with his fingers, and her hands were up at his shoulders and he was almost there and it killed to not be inside her.

'Ava?'

She looked up into green eyes and there was not a doubt in her mind and she nodded, resumed their kiss because she'd made up her mind.

'Hold on.' He went to get a condom, sure she'd insist on it—she'd even made him have blood tests and things, and only for Ava would he do that—but as she so often did, she surprised him. 'I've gone on the Pill.'

'Yeah, but…' He almost shrank from the responsibility, for about one tenth of a second, and then her hands slid over his back and down to his buttocks and he felt her mouth on his shoulder as he lowered himself and edged his way in, and she sobbed out at the delicious agony and there was a nip of her teeth on his shoulder that almost took him over the edge and then he met Ava, the real Ava that he'd unleashed, her kisses fervent, her words enticing, and his kisses and words were too.

It was sex that was worth waiting for. It was more than just sex that night in his bed.

'God, Ava…'

She heard him moan and she had to come, she could feel the urgency. She could not believe then the noise and the passion and the feel of him inside her, and she knew she'd take for ever, knew because she always had, except he was thrusting inside her, his entire body suddenly rigid, and she was the one uncoiled beneath him. She could hear her own moans, her own shouts, her own collapse into silence, and then back to the real world.

She lay in his arms, watching some strange foreign science fiction film on his television that had started, neither wanting to get up from their haven, happy to read the subtitles, at least until his mouth found her shoulder again.

They never had got to see the end…

''Night, Ava.'

He yawned and stood up at about halfway through the movie, and tonight James did bend to kiss her, not her mouth, but the top of her head, and she felt his fingers in her hair and for a second they lingered, but even as she turned her head to him, he lifted his and headed to bed, and as she heard the door click closed behind him she knew what had happened, thought about it quite logically for a moment, and then she cried.

That walk on the beach, the trip to Pete's and now the film.

He'd been saying goodbye.

CHAPTER TEN

'IT'S your mother on the phone.' Ginny had rung through.

Ava was about to tell Ginny that she was in with a client, but instead she asked that she be put through. 'You might as well go now, Ginny. I've just got a quick phone consultation and then I'm heading home,' Ava said, then took a breath and took the call from her mum.

'Hi, there,' Ava said.

'Hi, Ava.' Fleur wasn't really one for chatting. 'Any news on James?'

'Nothing yet,' Ava said, because they weren't expecting the results till next week and she wasn't sure that they were even going to make it to next week. She had been on the edge of tears between every patient, had the most appalling feeling in her stomach and all she wanted was to go home.

'Well, let your father and I know when you hear.' There was a slight pause. 'How are you?'

'I've been better,' Ava admitted. 'Actually, Mum…' And then she stopped herself because she was not going to discuss this with her mother and, anyway, Fleur wouldn't understand—her parents' marriage was so liberal and open, she could never understand what Ava was grappling with, aside from James's illness.

Still, maybe she could do with a dose of liberality, Ava thought, maybe she could try talking with her mum. Her mum wouldn't turn a hair if she told her she thought James had had an affair, was still having one.

Turn a blind eye would be her mother's advice. It was strange really, everyone thought Ava was so open-minded, so liberal, except she only was with James. She really did believe in love and was so proud of the couples that came to see her and worked through things. Yes, maybe she did need some of her mum's rather more open views. 'I was thinking I might come over and see you this weekend.'

'Oh!' She could hear the surprise in her mother's voice. 'Is he up and about, then?'

'Not with James,' Ava said. Perish the thought, James didn't exactly like her parents, had said in some rows how they'd messed her up, and the thought of them together with tensions so high didn't particularly appeal. 'Just me. I'll see how the next couple of days go and let you know.'

'Well, ring first,' Fleur warned. 'I don't want you driving all that way if I'm out.'

She was thoughtful like that, Ava refelected darkly, putting down the phone and resting her head in her hands. For all Veronica irritated her at times, at least she was there. All the Carmichael clan had been around and had it been Ava they would have done the same. Well, maybe it would be a slightly diluted version and maybe the fridge would be more full so that James wouldn't starve while she was incapacitated, but at least they would have stepped up.

Her mother hadn't so much as sent a card or even spoken to James.

Ava had never been close to her mother, or her father. The only person in her life she'd been really close to had been James.

'Ava.' There was a knock at the door and she looked up at his voice. Oh, God, he was wearing those grey linen pants and that black shirt and he'd shaved and he had on that cologne and he looked more beautiful than he ever had, more beautiful than the man she had married even, and she was gripped tighter with the fear that was ever-present these days. Because he couldn't be sick, he just couldn't be, and Ava knew why he was there but she asked just the same.

'What are you doing here?'

'Blake got my results in.'

'Already? That is really quick. When are you seeing him…?' Her voice trailed off, knew it was pointless, knew that James wasn't there to ask her to come along with him to find out the news.

'It's good news,' James said, and he went a bit technical for a moment. Yes, it was good news, it just wasn't quite as good as he had hoped, not quite as contained, but it was still stage one. As he explained, her mind couldn't keep up with him and he toned it down. 'I've gone through it all with Blake and I'm going to have a course of chemo. I want to know that it's gone.'

It wasn't a discussion, but that was fair enough, it was James's field after all. 'I'll still be working, I'll just have to schedule around it…' And he spoke a little more about what was involved and there was thin relief because the news could have been so much worse. But there was also a sense of fear of the unknown too, because so much had changed in such a short space of time.

'We'll get through it,' Ava said.

And he shook his head and she knew, really knew, why he was there, and a fear of the known closed in.

She'd known since last night that this was coming.

'I'm moving out.' He said it just like that. 'I'm going round to Mum's now to give her the results and to tell her that I've walked out.'

'Please, don't.' She knew that he meant it, knew he had made up his mind, could feel him slipping away, or rather that he had been slipping away for ages but now, at this moment, he was completely out of her grasp. 'James, please. This isn't the time to be making these sorts of decisions.'

'It's done,' James said. 'I've got a serviced apartment; I've just been and picked up the keys.'

'You're not supposed to be driving.'

'Yeah, well, I was looking on the internet and I found out that there were these yellow things called taxis…'

She hated it when he did this, when he just blocked her out.

'I want to be with you. I want to help you get through it.'

Except she'd blocked him out too, and he told her as much. 'Do you think I didn't want to be with you?' James said. 'Relationships are supposed to be a two-way street, but not ours. Your grief was too private, too deep to share with me—well, you can't just suddenly decide now that you want to be all open and touchy-feely.'

And she stood in her office where she fixed and she healed, where she let couples discuss and say the words that hurt to hear but needed to be said. Except with James it was final. James didn't want to be in here. Unlike her couples, James didn't want it fixed.

'I've taken what I need for now. I'll sort out the study and stuff when I can lift and things, but I'll arrange a time that's suitable with you.' He walked over and put his key on the table and he made it sound so terribly simple, except it was far from that. And then he took off his ring.

Well, she wasn't taking off hers.

'I'm not getting a lawyer,' Ava said. 'I don't want a divorce.'

'Of course you don't,' James said. 'It would be a bit of a stupid thing to do now.'

'Sorry?'

'All the life insurance and everything.'

'Oh, for God's sake…' She was so angry. 'You can be such a bastard.'

And he didn't try and stop the row this time, neither did he lean over to kiss her. He just headed for the door.

'You could go to your mum's.' She was frantic. Anything was better than a serviced apartment. She couldn't stand for him to go through this alone, but she knew him too well, knew his answer almost before it came.

'I don't want to go to my mum's. I don't want anyone near. I want the dignity to puke in private.'

CHAPTER ELEVEN

'HOW are you doing, James?'

It was two weeks later and he was sitting in a reclining chair, rather than standing beside it, as Harriet, one of the nurses he knew well, ran through the forms.

James hated paperwork, completely loathed it, but it had never dawned on him that the patients felt the same. He'd answered the same questions over and over, five minutes apart at times.

And always the answers had been the same.

Today, though, a few were different and as he skimmed through the form with Harriet, before he had his first round of treatment, he paused.

'My emergency contact has changed.'

'Oh.'

'It's Veronica Carmichael—my mother.' He made a thin joke. 'But only ring her if I'm dead—she worries a lot.'

And he had to change his home address too and delete his home phone number to bit by bit extract himself from Ava's life.

He'd seen Harriet many times all gloved and gowned up, but it felt very different to be sitting a reclining chair, getting his treatment. She'd done his obs diligently throughout and had chatted a little, but things *were* different. He found it very hard to pinpoint—his patients had spoken to him often about it and now he fully understood. There was this air of sympathy, of forced normality in almost every exchange he had these days, and James couldn't stand it. Sure, he preferred that Harriet wasn't flirting now, it had been awkward at times, but it wasn't about Harriet, it was about everyone. Well, almost everyone. There were still some people with whom he could relax.

'When you said you'd be beside me, whatever I decide…' James turned at the sound of Richard's—his teenage patient's—voice and gave a wry smile as he chatted on. 'This really is going above and beyond the call of duty.'

'I do my best,' James quipped back. 'Well, I guess you got your answer as to what I'd do if it was me.' He smiled at his patient and peer. 'Sorry I missed your appointment.' He really was. He knew how disappointed Richard would have been.

'No problem,' Richard said. 'I actually came back a couple of days after we spoke. I'd decided that I couldn't stand just waiting to see what happened. Blake said you weren't well—he didn't say what was wrong.' Richard looked him right in the eye. 'I'm really sorry.'

And they spoke about their results and their treatments.

'This is your second?' James glanced up

to the bag that was dripping its contents into Richard's arm. 'How was it?'

Richard pulled a face. 'Not as bad as I thought,' Richard said, 'but I've heard it gets worse.'

They spoke for a bit then Richard put his headphones on and listened to some music and when James got sick of the nurses chatting behind the glass—first about him. Did they know he and Ava had broken up? Later about Finn, how much he'd improved, but his arm was practically numb and there was some weakness in one of his legs. But he was insisting on being discharged apparently. He watched a DVD, a war one because he was sick of all the inspirational ones that people kept pressing on him. Still, even if it was a good movie, he couldn't really concentrate and instead he thought about many things as he tried not to think about Ava.

The cleaner was coming to the apartment

today, but he'd told her not to come for the next three. He'd had his hair cut really short, because he didn't want to scare her when it all fell out. He thought about the gym and how pleased he was that he was a bit fitter than if it had happened a few months ago, but he wished too he'd eaten better. He'd ordered some frozen meals, healthy ones, the ones that got delivered—but he felt like a fighter pilot scrambling when it was already too late.

'James!' Cleo, the charge nurse, had come in for her late shift and the second she saw him she was over as Harriet removed his IV. 'How are you doing?'

'I'm fine. Just about ready to go home.'

He didn't feel fine, actually. He knew everyone reacted differently but, in fact, for the first time since he'd found that lump he felt ill, as if they'd administered an IV labelled fatigue straight into him.

He had some tea and sandwiches and was

ready now to go home, or rather to return to the serviced apartment, but he couldn't stop thinking about the apartment at Kirribilli, about the fridge there that made ice cubes and the bed that was his, and he was still trying not to think about Ava.

'Did you want me to ring through to Ava and tell her you're ready for the off?' Cleo asked, and he saw Harriet's cheeks pink up

'No.' James shook his head. 'I just rang my mum and she's picking me up.' He'd had his anti-emetics, all the drugs dispensed, and he just wanted this over with.

'Ava and I broke up, Cleo.'

'Oh!' He watched as she struggled for a response. 'But you're at your mum's tonight?'

He didn't need a babysitter and they didn't need to know.

'Here she is.' James stood as Veronica entered. He saw the frantic look that had been on his mother's face since he'd first broken the news and he hated that he had put it there. 'Hey, Mum. Ready to go?'

Ava's mum wasn't worried. 'I'm not with you, Ava!' She'd done what she had said she never would and had gone to her mum's one lunchtime in the hope of advice. 'Ava, you haven't been sleeping together, you've been living separate lives, and now you're "devastated" that it's over?'

'You don't understand.'

'It's guilt, Ava.' Fleur was adamant. 'James had his chemo today and the martyr in you feels you ought to be there.'

And Ava listened, but not really, because her mum, she realised, just didn't do love.

'And whatever you do,' her mum said as she saw her to the car, 'don't even think about getting a divorce. No, don't look at me like that, Ava. I'm just being practical—you'd be mad to divorce him now, wouldn't you?'

Ava knew James had chemo today, and the day had stretched for ever, which was maybe why she had gone to her mum's. Sometimes she saw him at work, not often, but she'd started to have lunch in the canteen because so too had James. He'd had his hair cut short, in anticipation of the drug side effects, no doubt, but for now he looked as if he was brimming with health. He ignored her whenever he saw her, and one time she'd seen him sitting chatting with one of the nurses. Previously, she'd have just walked right on over, but instead she'd sat brittle and jealous, bobbing around in limbo—separated not divorced. Married but apart.

She walked through the car park, tried to focus her mind back on work, but really she would have preferred to go home and to bed and just pull the covers over her head. She had never felt more tired in her life.

It had been two weeks since he'd left her, and in those weeks Ava had grimly continued on as if it hadn't happened, as if James hadn't left. Desperately trying to convince herself that telling others would be premature—that any day now James would change his mind, that he'd ring and say he was on his way back home, or that she'd come out of the lift to find him waiting at the front door.

Apart from her mother this lunchtime, Ava hadn't told anybody. Amazingly for SHH, whose grapevine was legendary, word didn't seem to have got out yet. People were still asking her how James was doing, and after all she was still wearing her ring, and maybe James hadn't told anyone either. Maybe he was going to come back to her.

Ava forced herself to keep busy. She swam in the morning and rode most evenings, her time on the horse the only time her head felt calm, and then it was back to the flat that was too empty without him and a night spent resisting the urge to call.

Tonight would be even harder. She could not stand that he would be going through this treatment without her, and then she saw him, at the other end of the corridor and walking towards her. He looked the same as he had the last time she'd glimpsed him. Only Ava could see his exhaustion as James and Veronica neared. It was the first time in all of this that he actually looked unwell, or was it stress that marred his features? She truly didn't know.

At first he pretended not to have noticed her and Ava did the same, walking towards him with her heart hammering in her chest, pretending to check her phone, wondering how she should greet him. Veronica didn't look so well either—she seemed to have aged a decade since James had found the lump.

'Ava.' He nodded by way of a greeting, and she opened her mouth to speak to him to ask him how it had been, how he was feeling, except James wasn't in the mood for conversation and had already walked on.

'Hi, there, Ava.' Ginny gave her a smile as she walked past the desk and with supreme effort she gave her one back. 'Is everything okay?' Ginny asked. 'You're ever so pale.'

'I'm fine,' Ava said when she felt like screaming, and somehow she made it to her office.

Somehow she made it through the afternoon, but for once her mind could not quite focus on her patients. She did her best, of course, maybe they didn't notice, but in truth her mind was with James and her body ached to sleep.

She should be in bed this minute beside him, for she knew that that was where he would have headed, and it was as if her body was insisting, as if it was demanding that that be where she should be too.

'See you, Ginny.' For once she left on the stroke of five, hitched up her bag and said goodnight.

'Oh!' Ginny looked up from whatever she was doing. 'See you, Ava…' Except it was Ginny who forced the smile this time and Ava knew then that she knew.

That word was out.

That James and Ava's marriage was over.

Yes, there was guilt, but it was only a part of how she felt as she headed for home, as she stood in the lift, which was working tonight, then let herself in the door.

Even if she'd lived alone for three months, it had still been James's home. There had still been the *chance* that he'd come home, but now it just felt empty.

Now would come the appalling silence from friends while they worked out what best to say. She and James had been guilty of that when Donna and Neil had split up.

'Ring him,' Ava had pushed.

'Ring her,' James had pushed.

They'd worried so much as to whom to ring

first, in the end she'd gone into the bedroom and James to his study and they'd both rung at the same time on their mobiles and then met back in the lounge for a good old gossip.

She wasn't ready yet to smile at the memory. Smiling felt a long way off—at least in her personal life—and she knew it was pathetic to hope when there was a knock at the door, except she did.

'Oh, Ava.' It was Evie at her door

'You've heard the happy news, then.' She pulled the door open and let Evie in.

'I don't know what to say,' Evie admitted. 'I've been banging on about my problems and all this time…'

'Don't worry about that,' Ava said. 'It's nice of you to come over—it's been pretty chilly at the hospital this afternoon.' She made them both a drink, this time, though, it was for Ava to compose herself for a moment. 'So what's the gossip?' Ava asked when they were both sitting down. 'What's everyone saying?'

'Just that you two have split up. I actually heard something last week, but I just ignored it. I mean I know how hap—' She halted herself. 'I thought you two were so happy, it's just assumed that you are really,' Evie said. 'And what with James being sick, it seemed ridiculous. I knew you'd never…' She felt Evie glance at her wedding-ring finger, the ring still firmly there.

'He left me,' Ava said, but she knew that probably wasn't what was being said. 'Anyway, I don't have to defend myself.'

'Of course you don't.'

'I don't mean to you.' Ava shook her head, couldn't believe the mess her life was. 'We've been having problems for a long time.' Ava let out a little of what for so long she had been holding in. 'It isn't completely out of the blue. It just feels that way, though,' Ava admitted. It was actually nice to have Evie over, she was far easier to talk to than her own mother, and it was a relief to find out a bit about James.

'He's taking the next couple of days off, I think,' Evie said. 'The courses of chemo are three weeks apart, well, that's what I've heard.'

'I don't know anything,' Ava admitted. 'I don't know how bad it's going to be.' They chatted for a while about James and then Ava warmed them both a frozen meal for one and she asked after Finn.

'It doesn't look great,' Evie said. 'Not that I'm allowed to know.'

'He's still not letting you visit?'

'He's not letting anyone visit,' Evie said. 'You know he had some swelling after the operation and that's subsided, but…' Ava felt as if she were looking in a mirror. She could see the lines of tension around Evie's eyes, see the set of her lips as she struggled to stay positive. 'Well, things aren't great, but he's going home tomorrow and there's talk of scheduling another operation…'

They both stopped as they heard noises from above, like an angry ghost of Finn, because they were talking about him, but then Evie laughed.

'That's Luke and Lily,' Evie said. 'Luke prised his key off him and they're sorting out things there tonight, you know, fitting a shower chair and things…' Ava could see the sparkle of tears in Evie's eyes. 'He'll hate that.'

'Better than a wheelchair,' Ava said.

'I think Luke's gone and got another key cut so he can keep an eye on him, and they're stocking up the fridge,' Evie said, 'hiding the Scotch.'

Ava glanced up at the almost full bottle still sitting on the bench and thought about that night. For all they said about Finn's reckless ways, he could be very sensible too. 'He'll just bribe Gladys if he wants some.' Ava smiled. 'Finn's gong to be okay.'

'You don't know that,' Evie said.

But she did. Somewhere deep inside, she just felt that Finn would be okay. She just wished she had the same feeling about James.

Evie went up to help Lily and Luke, but Ava simply couldn't handle any more company or sympathy tonight and after she said farewell to Evie she took a long shower. She was too tired to blow-dry her hair so instead she did the hardest thing.

Took off her ring for the first time in seven years.

She'd felt Evie looking at her ring finger and now she thought about it, Ginny had too. She felt like the relatives days after an earthquake, still insisting the emergency workers keep looking, still demanding there was hope, when it had all but faded. Except she couldn't leave it there by the sink, so she added it to the chain she wore around her neck and she crawled into bed and lay there wondering how he was feeling tonight.

She didn't even try not to think about James.

The first wave of nausea hit at 5:00 a.m.

Just this violent wave, the type that jolted you awake and propelled you out of bed, and then a frantic dash to the bathroom and the chill of cold sweat as you knelt in the dark because you didn't have time to switch on the light.

Ava clung to the toilet bowl and held on for dear life, wondering if she was having sympathy nausea with James, because she hadn't vomited since…

She closed her eyes as another wave hit and then she started to cry because she simply couldn't be pregnant. They'd had sex once, for God's sake. She was on the Pill, except she hadn't taken it the morning they found the lump, and perhaps not the morning after that too.

Ava was terrified she was pregnant.

Refused to be.

She had gastric flu, she decided, and for the first time in a very long time she rang in at eight and used some of her sick leave, made a cup of tea and went back to bed.

Then she woke up at ten-thirty and couldn't dress quickly enough in her haste to find out. She walked down to the chemist, which had once been her regular walk—a monthly walk where she'd buy two pregnancy kits that each contained two pregnancy tests, because if it was negative she'd want to do it again the next morning and the morning after that too, and if it was positive, she'd be taking the test again and again just to be sure.

She bought one that morning.

One single one and then walked back to the flat, cursing her timing because there were Luke and Lily trying to hold back as a very thin and dishevelled Finn dragged himself on a cane towards the lift, his arm hanging limp and useless beside him.

'Morning.' She gave Lily and Luke an attempt at a smile and was completely ignored by Finn.

She felt as if they had X-ray vision and could see through the paper bag she was holding but knew that, in truth, they were thinking of Finn.

'Ava.' Lily returned her smile. 'I was going to call you.' She was just a little bit awkward and who could blame her? 'We should catch up…'

'Sure,' Ava replied, relieved when the lift door opened and she let herself into the flat and raced to the loo. She waited, desperate for the first time for the result to be negative.

She couldn't do this again.

Not now.

Not alone.

And how could she put James through it too?

She cried so hard when she saw that cross and she truly didn't know what to do. Except he had to know, he deserved to know, surely. And now there was a legitimate reason to see him too.

She drove to his serviced apartment and knocked on the door, bracing herself to be honest, to talk it out as she told all her clients, except it was Veronica who answered the door and her face was savage.

'What the hell do you want?'

'My husband,' Ava said.

'He's been up all night, ill,' Veronica said. 'He's told me that if you come to the door that you're not to be allowed in.'

'Look, Veronica.' Ava tried to keep her voice even. 'I need to speak to him.'

'Well, James doesn't need to speak to you, he doesn't need the stress…' Veronica said, and then she took her out into the hall and closed the door behind her. 'What sort of woman would leave her husband at a time like this?'

'He left me!' Ava reminded her, but she knew

it was hopeless, knew the gossip around the hospital, and it was the same here—she was the shrew who couldn't stand by her man, who had got out when the going got tough.

'He stood by you through all those miscarriages,' Veronica hissed. 'Whatever your problems were, could you not have put them on hold?'

'I just need to talk to him.'

'Well, the last thing he needs right now is you,' Veronica said. 'And I mean it, Ava. I bought him some DVDs and we've just been watching them. The best thing, they say, is to stay positive—James needs to be concentrating on himself not trying to repair a marriage that's been over for more than a year.' She must have seen Ava's already pale face turn to chalk. 'Just let him concentrate on himself.'

And she had to put it on hold, Ava realised, not just the marriage but the pregnancy too—

she could not add to the pressure that James was under right now.

What was she supposed to tell him? *Oh, darling, I'm pregnant!* She knew the hell that would cause him, the confusion and fear, that James would know what she was going through, that somehow he would feel that he had to support her too as he did his best to get through his treatment.

And how could she tell him tomorrow or next week or next month that she'd lost it? How could she add to it all?

'If I were you—' Veronica broke into her trance '—if you care about him at all, you will just leave him well enough alone.'

CHAPTER TWELVE

IT WAS hell to see him suffer from a distance.

He dragged himself to work, and over the weeks he lost weight, of course, but actually bald suited him. He carried right on working and sometimes she saw him laughing and chatting with colleagues, but only once did he meet her eyes. She was buying a coffee in the canteen and looked up to his and he didn't tear them away. Instead, he made his way over.

'I need to get a few things.'

'Sure.' She felt as if everyone in the canteen was watching them. 'When did you want to come over?'

'Tonight,' James said. 'Unless you're busy?'

'Tonight's fine.'

And, though tonight might be the time to tell

him, she knew she wouldn't, for while it *was* hell to see him suffer from a distance, there was also a sense of relief too.

He had enough to deal with and it was better that he wasn't burdened with the worry about the pregnancy, that he wasn't walking on egg-shells and worrying about her and how she'd be if she lost it. It actually felt easier for Ava, too, because she wasn't worrying about how disappointed he'd be when she did.

Except she didn't.

And it was starting to show.

So she pulled on leggings and a big sloppy jumper, not that she was really showing, but she was rounding out a bit and she worried he might notice.

He came over as arranged at eight.

Ava had wondered if it would be four mates and a truck, but it was just James.

'It's just mainly books that I came for,' James said, noting her attire, just a little bit annoyed that she hadn't made any effort at all. 'And clothes…' His were hanging off him. 'I've got some jeans from before I put on weight.'

'I threw them out.'

'Well, that didn't take long.'

'I threw them out years ago,' Ava said. 'You couldn't have worn them anyway—they would be totally out of fashion!' She hauled open the wardrobes and found some of his old black jeans that were a couple of sizes smaller and James took some T-shirts and then he went to the study.

'Do you want something to eat?' Ava offered.

'No, don't go to any trouble,' he called.

'It's no trouble,' Ava called back as she walked to the study. 'I could ring out for pizza.'

Except he'd given up pizza, was trying so hard to stick to the promises he'd made to himself deep into the night.

'No, really, I'm fine.'

'Coffee, then?'

She'd laugh if he told her he was drinking green tea.

'A glass of water would be great.' And she thought he was snubbing her while he thought of the fridge that pumped cold water and the sound of ice cubes as they hit the glass and wondered if he'd be pushing things if he asked for custody of the fridge.

'Here.' She handed him the glass and as he drank it down she forced conversation. 'How have you been doing?'

'Oh, you know,' James said. 'Chemo has its fun side.'

'Such as?'

'I can't think right now.' He was at his sarcastic best. 'How annoying is that? Oh, but it's right there on the tip of my tongue.'

'That bad, then?'

He just shrugged and carried on filling a box, and then he was done and their wedding photo was still sitting on the study desk. He hadn't added that to the mix.

'Donna came over,' Ava said. 'She rang for a chat last weekend and then got annoyed that I hadn't told her.' Ava rolled her eyes. 'Honestly, I need a to-do list!'

'Neil rang,' James said. 'Donna must have told him. I think he thought we'd be hitting the clubs together, he wasn't too impressed when he found out about the cancer.' Then he looked over. 'How was Donna?'

'Still talking about Neil.' Somehow they laughed. 'Still *moaning* about Neil. I wanted to put my hand up and stop her,' Ava said. 'I wanted to say, er, my marriage *just* broke up, yours ended years ago…'

And it shouldn't concern him, it was none of his business really, but he did want to know. 'How did your parents take it?'

'Oh,' Ava answered. 'Mum suggested I moved into my old bedroom so she could mother me a bit, you know…' And he stood and he looked because she didn't need to say she was being sarcastic, and even if his own mum drove him crazy at times he couldn't stand the way Ava's family were with her. It would be so easy now to wrap his arms around her, to stay, to just give in, but pride was a wall he couldn't get through.

'I think that's everything.'

He walked out into the living room and he could see the hospital and see the harbour and the view he knew and it smelt like home and he didn't want to go back to the serviced apartment and to sheets that smelt vaguely of bleach. He wanted to go right now and lie down in the bedroom that had once been theirs and just close his eyes, or even just rest on the sofa, except he had another treatment due soon, and it didn't exactly make for tender reunions. And, after all, she hadn't wanted him when he was well.

'If there's anything else you want…?'

'The fridge,' James said.

'Ha, ha.' She tried to laugh as he walked to the door and then she said what was true. 'I miss you.'

And he couldn't not ask. 'How are you doing?'

'I don't know,' Ava admitted. She truly didn't know. She wasn't teary any more, she was glad he wasn't worrying about her and the pregnancy on top everything else. And she only thought about his cancer for fifty-five minutes of every hour now, which was an improvement on the previous week. It was funny how with James she could sometimes be her most honest. 'I'm tired,' Ava said. 'I'm the most tired I've ever been.'

'And me.'

He was, and always had been the only person who could ever really comfort her, not all the time, of course, because too often she hadn't let him, but tonight she did. He put down the box and he pulled her into his arms and let her rest there for a little while, and he rested there too.

'Come back, James,' she said to his chest.

'I can't,' James said to her hair that smelt of lavender and somehow, in the hallway, not looking, just holding, he was able to be honest, the most honest he had been with anyone since he'd found that lump. He knew that he was too proud for his own good, knew that he could be stubborn at times, but he felt as if he'd been given a golden ticket. Only it was one he didn't want, one that excused all previous behaviour, resolved all rows, that now he was sick, only now was he wanted. And he didn't want a marriage built on her guilt, didn't want to drag her along for the appalling ride when they'd already been about to get off.

'I can't come back, Ava. Let me do this myself.' But, yes, so badly he missed her and it wasn't just pride that stopped him. There was something else too. His mortality had been rammed home to him, and while the statistics were good…

Better to lose him this way, the dark nights told him.

Better that she get over him now, because surely Ava did not deserve another loss. And he found himself kissing her and she kissed him back. A deep, lingering kiss that neither of them wanted to end because then they'd have to confront it, so they just carried on kissing and let their mouths speak a language that was safer than words at the moment. When it ended she put her face back against his chest, a bit embarrassed and confused at the want that was still in them.

'I've got to go,' James said, still holding her.

And she didn't fight it, because she understood that he did.

But it was nice to hold on to each other for a moment.

CHAPTER THIRTEEN

SOMETIMES, Ava now realised, talking *was* impossible.

In fact, as the weeks went on she revised one of her well-worn theories, not just for herself but for her patients too.

'It's good to see you again,' she said as she stepped into the waiting room to call her next patients in.

It really was a joy to see George and Elise—to see all of her patients, in fact. She loved her work, no matter how Veronica or others might sniff or nudge; she loved seeing the difference she made.

Today it was a visible difference as she stepped out into her waiting room and saw Elise smiling and George walking into her office, of course a little awkward, but she'd heard them talking and laughing as she'd gone for their file. She knew before they had even sat down how much better things were for them—it was evident in their body language, in the smiles that greeted her.

And during the consultation she found out she was right.

Right in several ways, in fact!

'I just wish we'd come to see you sooner,' Elise said.

'Well, a lot of couples say that,' Ava admitted. 'They struggle on their own for a very long time, not realising that there's help available.'

'I just wish George had told me all he was going through. I could have helped…'

'Maybe George needed to do that by himself,' Ava said gently. 'Maybe he needed to work things out on his own.'

'But you say we should talk…'

'I know I do,' Ava said, 'but sometimes, when

talking doesn't help, all you can rely on is time to heal and your history to hold you together while things sort themselves out. George had a lot of things to deal with, a lot of things to get straight in his own mind before he was able to share. And now look at you—your relationship seems better than it was even before the accident.' And it seemed strange that from something so terrible any good could come, but with George and Elise it had. 'I'd like to see you both again in three months. I also just want to check your medication, George, and I do want to see you again on your own, say, in another month?'

George nodded. He was going back to work in a couple of months, and Ava wanted to make sure he was ready for it.

'Well, it's been lovely to see you both again.' Ava saw them to the door.

'It's been lovely to see you too, Ava!' Elise

gave her a smile, a knowing smile perhaps? 'You're looking very well.'

'Thank you.' Ava went a bit pink and she felt as if Elise knew.

Maybe Elise did. After all Ava had a white shirt on that was straining just a little at the top buttons, her waist was getting thicker, and just this morning she hadn't been able to do up her skirt. There was certainly a roundness there, and her bottom was a bit bigger too—the first subtle changes of pregnancy becoming more evident now. She was also further on than she had ever been, which was bizarre. She was swimming, working, stressing, crying, she hadn't even seen a doctor—after all, it hadn't helped in the past, but now… Ava knew that she ought to. She was taking vitamins, looking after herself, but she really ought to get checked.

Her phone rang and she was about to let it

go to messages and get some lunch, but she reached for it instead.

'Ava Carmichael.'

'Ava, this is Marco, I am working today in outpatients.' A rich Italian accent came down the phone as he introduced himself—but of course she knew who he was. The dashing Italian obstetrician who was married to Emily, a midwife here. Serendipity, Ava thought with a wry smile, but of course he was ringing to discuss a patient.

'She is four months pregnant through IVF, her husband is paraplegic—they are the most delightful couple, but on speaking to them today, I feel there is not enough information for them. They are both from the country so there is not much help available. Could I arrange for you to see them, or one of your colleagues? Of course I will write a referral, but I worry that if I make them wait…'

'Strike while the iron's hot, you mean?'

'Scusi?'

Ava smiled. He clearly didn't understand what she was saying. 'I'll come over now.'

After meeting with the young couple, she was actually thrilled that Marco had phoned her and a bit appalled at the lack of information the pair had been struggling with. Barry's accident had happened when he was twelve and there was a whole lot he hadn't been informed about. A shy couple, they had at first been terribly reluctant to speak—but once they had started, a full hour had flown by, and she rang Ginny to make an appointment to coincide with their next antenatal visit, delighted to have been able to help.

'Ava!' She smiled when she saw Bella in the waiting room.

'Look at you!' Ava said, because Bella was looking very glamorous. 'How's the studying going?'

'I'm wearing it today,' Bella said. She was studying fashion and looked gorgeous and happy, having recently married. 'So what are you doing here?' Bella nudged.

'Working!' Ava grinned. 'What about you.'

'Just here to find out a few things. I'm waiting for Charlie but I got here a bit early.' She gave a little blush. 'We're thinking of starting a family and given all my medications and things, we just need to find stuff out. So please don't go gossiping!'

'As if!' Ava rolled her eyes.

'I heard about you and James,' Bella said. 'Felt sick when I heard.'

'Thanks,' Ava said, because she felt sick about it too. 'Anyway, I've got to go, I just need to pop in and thank Marco, but you take very good care of yourself. I hope today goes well.'

'You take care of yourself too, Ava,' Bella said, and as Ava headed to Marco's room and saw the door open she knew that Bella was right, and she knocked and popped in and introduced herself.

'Marco, hi, it's Ava, from the sexual dysfunction clinic.'

'Ah, Ava.' He gave her a very nice smile.

'Thank you for the referral. I've had a long talk with them and I'll be seeing them again. I think it's been really helpful.'

'No. Thank you,' Marco said. 'I was very pleased to have this resource, it was very confident of them to speak.'

He meant courageous, but confidence, courage, it was all the same in a way and it was exactly what she needed to summon now.

'Can I speak to you?' She stepped into the office, closing the door behind her. 'About me.'

'Of course.'

'Off the record?'

Marco gave a nod.

'Your wife's a midwife here.'

'Your husband is an oncologist who is undergoing chemotherapy.' Marco said. 'I know what this place is like and you can rest assured that you are speaking only with me.'

'I'm pregnant,' Ava said, and it was a relief to say it. 'But the thing is…' she swallowed '…my husband doesn't know—we're separated.'

'It's his?' Marco checked.

'Oh, yes.' Ava nodded. 'And I know I should have told him—it's just that I've had four miscarriages and it's been hell. We were already separated when I found out and I couldn't stand to do it to him again when I knew it was going to end up the same way…'

'But it hasn't?'

'No.'

And she explained about her previous pregnancies and the investigations that had taken place. 'There was nothing to explain it—all the tests came back as NAD…'

'How far along did you get?'

'Ten weeks was the longest.' Ava said. 'We

decided, or rather I decided, that I didn't want to get pregnant again. It was just too hard to go through.' It was such a relief to talk and Marco didn't rush her. 'It put an incredible strain on our marriage…'

'I can imagine.'

'I thought that by going on the Pill…' She could feel tears welling, and really she didn't want to start crying but was grateful when he peeled off some tissues and handed them to her.

'I'm sorry.'

'Please don't be—I see many tears here every day. Do you know how far along you are?

She gave him the date of her last period and he checked on his calendar.

'That puts you at fourteen weeks,' Marco said. 'Into your second trimester. Let's have a look, shall we?'

She went over to the examination table and he took her blood pressure and then he took it again. 'It's at the higher end of normal.' Marco gave her the numbers.

'I'm a bit tense.'

'Of course, and I've taken that into consideration, but I'd like to keep an eye on that. I don't want it going any higher if we can help it.' Then Marco felt her bump and she had a bump, not a big one but certainly there was a small bump.

And then he put a disc into the scanner. 'Let's make a recording.'

And she looked and wished so badly that James was here, because there was their baby on the screen and it really was a baby and she was very scared to look because she knew she'd fall in love.

'It looks every bit as good as I could hope,' Marco said. 'The placenta is nice and high, the measurements are spot on and the heart rate is good.' He went through everything as she lay there, not really sure how she felt, and then he helped her up and she went and sat down at his desk. They spoke for a few minutes about antenatal care and she confessed to two swigs of whisky and a glass of wine and horse riding before she'd found out, but Marco just smiled.

'I don't recommend women take up horse riding when pregnant, but if you are a competent rider, many women ride all the way through, and if it relaxes you…' He reached for his pen. 'We should do some bloods too.'

'Can they wait?' Ava said, and maybe she was being paranoid but she didn't want it documented till she had shared things with James.

'Of course,' Marco said. 'But can I suggest you don't wait too long.'

'I've been taking vitamins—'

'Ava,' Marco interrupted, 'I'm not worried about your bloods at the moment. The fact is, maybe I am a little more perceptive about these things than most men, but I knew you were pregnant as soon as you walked in—your husband will be perceptive in this too. He'll see for himself in a week or two.'

And then he spoke some more and he mentioned something that James had on several occasions, something she had baulked at, something that had caused the most terrible rows.

'I haven't been depressed,' Ava insisted. 'I've just been dealing with a lot.'

'Of course—you have been dealing with many things,' Marco said. 'But depression is something I like to speak openly about, especially with women who have suffered losses.'

Ava nodded in all the right places and then thanked him for his care and told him that soon she would be in to see him formally, then headed down to the canteen, still clutching the DVD Marco had made for her.

She bought her lunch and then saw James walking in.

She watched as he moved his tray along the counter, and felt as if the world was watching as he sat at a table far from her. He looked better than he had for a while, but that only meant he had a treatment due soon then, because just as he seemed to pick up and get some colour, he was soon wiped out again.

How did she tell him?

She had the DVD on the table beside her. Maybe she should just walk over now, maybe she'd just give it to him and let him watch it in private. Let him work out himself how he felt, just as she was trying to do.

She watched as a nurse went and sat with him.

That cow, Ava thought, when things like that had never once troubled her.

'Hi, there.' Ava looked up at a smiling Lily.

'Mind if I join you?' Lily asked.

'Sure.' Ava gave an awkward smile. Lily was rather more pregnant than the last time she'd seen her. She was glowing, in fact, and Ava felt awful for her horrible thoughts on the day of James's operation. Not that Lily would know.

'How are you?' Lily asked.

'I've been better,' Ava admitted. 'I just feel as if everybody's watching us, everybody's wondering how I can not be with James as he goes through this.'

'Nobody's thinking that,' Lily said. 'If anybody's saying anything, it's just how awful it must be—for both of you.'

'Thanks,' Ava said, not that she really believed it—oh, maybe their friends thought that, but gossip could be so vicious and Ava hated it. 'And, Lily, I have to apologise—I wasn't very nice to you when James had his surgery.'

'What?' Lily clearly had no idea what Ava was talking about.

'I wasn't very friendly.'

Lily just laughed. 'I'm sure you had far more on your mind than worrying about being friendly to the nurse.'

'I know.' Ava shook her head. She should just let it go, but Lily was being so nice and she wanted to apologise properly. 'I was just in a horrible place that day. I was jealous that James had clearly spoken to you about his pain and…' she gave an awkward shrug '…that he had told you he wanted to stay in hospital rather than go home.' Lily said nothing, neither confirmed nor denied, just leant over and gave Ava's hand a squeeze.

'It was just everything—and with you being pregnant as well. I knew my marriage was over and the thing is, we lost some babies…' She was starting to tell people, but it was still so difficult. 'Hard to explain.'

'Easy to understand,' Lily said, and Ava gave a smile of thanks, grateful for Lily's kind words. 'You should come out to the farm, get away from everything for a bit,' Lily suggested.

Ava was about to shake her head, to decline as she always did these days. She was just too low to talk to anyone and too scared that if she did, she might reveal her secret before she told James, except getting away for a bit sounded so tempting. Lily and Luke had a gorgeous farm less than an hour away, she'd been to their wedding there and it had been glorious, and it was terribly tempting, and they had always said they should catch up.

'Luke's on call so it will just be us. Come for the weekend if you want.'

She wouldn't go for the weekend, Ava decided, but she did go over the next day.

First, though, she stopped by at Finn's.

She was sick of ignoring him, sick of pretending they'd never talked, so she bought a fresh filled roll from the baker's and two chocolate éclairs and then headed up to him.

'Finn.' She knocked at the door. 'It's Ava.' She knocked again, feeling awkward because clearly he didn't want to see her, or maybe he was out, maybe he was over at Evie's, so she ate the roll and packed up the éclairs, made the forty-minute drive to Luke and Lily's. It was so nice to get away from the hospital and the lonely flat.

Lily had made a picnic—a huge chicken, avocado and mango salad—and then packed it all into a basket with sparkling water and Ava's éclairs. They walked for a while and then sat down and basked in the lovely sunshine as they ate lunch. Lily was marvellous, just let her ramble a bit, because she'd found out that James *did* have another round of treatment on Monday and, of course, she was worried about that. As much as they talked, the two women said nothing at times too—just lay back on the grass after lunch. Lily's eyes closed, her lovely bump moving, and Ava's eyes open, wondering if she'd ever have a bump that moved too, wondering how James would take it when she told him.

But she couldn't now, could she?

Couldn't land this on him when he had a round of chemo booked.

'Do you want to walk?' Ava was suddenly panicked, but Lily just grinned and said sure, and they walked in the sun. Ava calmed a little and, yes, it was good to get away. 'Luke's uncle Tom has a property over there…' Lily pointed out the landmarks as they walked around late afternoon. 'He's wonderful.'

They turned into the stables and it was surely the most beautiful place on God's earth, because just the sounds and the smells had Ava relaxing.

'You've met Glenfiddich,' Lily said, and Ava stroked his mane. He was absolutely beautiful. 'He's the one I rode for the wedding.'

'He's gorgeous.'

'Luke thinks he's too spirited, but he's a baby really. We could go riding,' Lily suggested.

'You're still riding?' Ava asked, because Lily must be seven months pregnant now.

'I'd go mad if I didn't,' Lily said as they walked to the next stable. 'I've had all the lectures from Luke but I've told him that riding keeps my blood pressure down.

'This is Checkers.' Lily gave the old boy a kiss. He was huge—big and black with a white blaze—and Lily told her he had been Luke's when he was a kid. 'He's such a gentle old thing,' Lily said. 'We had some children visiting the other day who had never seen a horse before and Luke put one of them on him. He'd never startle—would you, Checkers?' And though she hadn't said, somehow Ava knew that Lily knew too. 'It's a privilege to ride you, isn't it, baby?' Lily crooned to Checkers.

'Can I?' Ava asked.

It didn't feel brave or risky to be back in the saddle—it felt right. In fact, Ava was quite sure that had there been a blood-pressure cuff attached to her arm now, the numbers would be tumbling down—she felt her heels push down and her pelvis move, felt the strength and the trust in the horse beneath her, and they walked on, mostly in silence, as Checkers did what horses did for Ava—cleared her head.

And she *did* end up staying the night. She and Lily watched a girly movie and ate chocolate as only two pregnant women really could. And they went riding again early in the morning and she cleared her head further still. Finally Ava was ready—to go home.

To think.

To be honest.

Not with James. First she had to be honest with herself.

James had been right and Marco too had been right to flag it.

Depression was such a cloaked thing and, no, she hadn't wanted to have it, hadn't wanted to face it, had refuted it when James had suggested she might be, had got angry when he had insisted she was.

And then she'd given up.

She'd given up so many things. They'd even eaten different meals, hers rich in folate and no raw fish or soft cheese, *just in case*, and she'd hated it when he'd shoved a Camembert in the oven and eaten it all melted. He'd done it the night after her last miscarriage, the night she'd thrown him out of her bed, the night he'd taken residence on the sofa and there he had stayed.

And she looked at those times through his eyes now.

He'd been trying to comfort her, making her a food that she loved, that they could cuddle up on the sofa and share. He just hadn't got how much it had hurt, how unpregnant that cheese had made her feel that night.

She looked through their wedding photos and through loads of albums, watched as her smile disappeared, oh, not in public, of course, but there were little clues in the images. James with his arm around her there at Lily and Luke's wedding. She was just so rigid beside him, and as she sat on the sofa, she recalled the terrible row of the night before. And she'd been so awkward that day because Finn had been best man and the miscarriage had happened just a few weeks before.

And there was Mia and Luca, so clearly besotted with each other as she and James stood slightly apart. She turned the pages and every one was a fresh memory. There she was with Hayley and Tom, and Ava actually smiled when she saw the photo, because he'd told her that day too not to pat the dog, and yet it hadn't felt like a snub then.

And there was Teo and Zoe's wedding photo, taken on the beach in Samoa, Teo so proud of his bride and loving Zoe's daughter as if she were his own.

James had tried to talk to her about fostering, adoption, but she'd been too scared of being let down.

She looked at her friends, saw Lexi and Sam unashamedly kissing. Those days had long since gone for James and herself.

She'd made it that way.

Ava knew that.

She'd refused to do the one thing she always told her patients they should.

To talk, to be honest, to get help if required. But then, James hadn't been honest either. James had kept it all in too, he'd just been this rock when she'd wanted his pain, and he'd hated it so much when she'd wept. He was an oncologist, for God's sake. He should be used to grief, used to pain.

Not hers, though…

She saw it then, that just as she wasn't the fabulous sex therapist at home, like everybody assumed, James was a different person at work too.

They knew what they were doing at work—it was the relationship part where they'd got lost.

And she wanted him home.

So badly.

Wanted to ring him, but didn't know what to say, didn't know where to start, wondered if he was in bed now, having his mind taken off things by this mysterious Steph woman, if she'd flown down from Brisbane…

She truly wondered if she'd left it too late.

There was a frantic thumping at the door and she ran to it. There was urgency in the knock, need, she was sure he could feel it, sure that finally it was James.

'Ava…' It was Gladys, the cleaner, her face ashen. 'I need help. It's Finn, I've just found him on the floor.'

CHAPTER FOURTEEN

GLADYS was too slow to wait for and Ava charged up the stairs.

She knew Gladys dropped in on Finn a lot and especially since he'd been out of the hospital.

'Oh, Finn.' She was appalled by what she saw—his breathing was terrible, rasping and rapid, and as she rolled him onto his side she could feel the heat from his clammy skin, saw the scar down his neck was angry and infected. How long had he been lying here? She cursed herself for yesterday morning. She should have kept knocking, or maybe rung Luke, but that was ridiculous. The last thing Finn wanted was a caretaker.

'Have you called an ambulance, Gladys?' Ava checked as the old lady puffed in.

'I didn't know what to do so I came and got you.'

'Okay, well, pass me the phone.'

Some doctor she was! She punched in the numbers and spoke to the operator. She didn't even have a bag, well, not one with anything that would help Finn at this moment! He was severely dehydrated and very, very ill, and the wait for the ambulance was interminable, especially with the hospital so close.

'I rang him earlier,' Gladys said. 'I'd made a nice roast and I thought I'd bring some for him, he's been losing so much weight.' She was beside herself. 'He didn't answer and I got all worried. I was nervous to let myself in…'

'Thank God that you did,' Ava said.

'What do you think is wrong with him?'

'He's got a wound infection,' Ava said. 'And a chest infection too by the sound of it.' She was furious with Finn, angry with this stubborn, proud man who just refused all help. 'There's nothing we can do till the ambulance gets here. Go down and get the lift ready for them.'

She thought of Evie, thought of how terrible it would be for her to have Finn come in in this condition if she was on duty tonight, and she used the phone again and asked to be put through to Emergency and then to the nurse in charge.

'No, I need to speak to the nurse in charge now.' She pulled rank. 'It's Dr Carmichael and it's about a patient that's being brought in.'

And the charge nurse, when she came to the phone, was lovely, she got it completely when Ava told her that the patient coming in soon was Finn.

'We'll get set up for him and I'll go and speak to Evie now,' the charge nurse said. 'Thanks so much for letting me know.'

The paramedics were marvellous. They put

in two drips and poured fluids into him and gave him oxygen too, and by the time they had moved him down and the cool night air hit, Finn was coming around just a little. She sat in the back of the ambulance with him for the short trip to SHH.

'Evie…' She knew he was worrying about the same thing as she had.

'She knows, Finn.' She'd never tried to be soft with him and she wouldn't start now, and anyway he wouldn't appreciate it. So she didn't hold his hand and make soothing noises. Instead she watched through the darkened window as the ambulance sped through the night and she was cross with Finn, so, so cross with him, and when he was better she'd tell him—in trying to save Evie from the burden, he'd just hurt her a whole lot more, Ava could see that.

Could see many things as they turned in to the approach for the hospital.

No matter how difficult it might make things, James really did need to know now.

She went to James's apartment straight from the hospital.

Finn was already improving, but Ava still felt faint at the thought of him lying on that floor all night because had Gladys not dropped in, he simply might not have been holding on by morning.

She wanted James, not just to tell him about the baby, not just to fight for them, but because tonight had been horrible and James was the only person who would understand the fright she'd had. She wasn't used to dealing with acute patients. It had been awful to feel so helpless.

Except he wasn't home, and she thought about ringing him, but sometimes you just needed face to face, so she waited it out all night and then in the morning she headed up to the oncology floor, prepared to wait in his office if she had to. To just close the door and have this out. But as she walked along the corridors she saw Evie. She didn't want to stop, but Evie clearly did.

'Ava! Thank you for last night.'

'It's no problem. Thank God for Gladys…'

Ava went to move on but Evie was still talking. She didn't want to hear about Finn, she wanted James. 'He's been treating the wound infection at home, can you believe it?' Evie was furious. 'Hasn't told anyone.' She let out a hiss of frustration as on and on she went when all Ava wanted was James. 'He's refusing to see anyone. Hayley wants to take him to Theatre for debridement, but he's refusing and he's told them to cancel the next operation. He wants to lecture instead of operate—'

'Evie…' Ava interrupted. She didn't want to hear about anyone else, she just wanted James. 'I'm sorry but I have to go.' She was almost running. She just wanted to see her husband. She took the lift to Oncology, except the lift let her out on the wrong floor, on the surgical ward, and just as she was about to go back in when she changed her mind because as desperately as she wanted to see James, there was something about the lifts not working and Finn, something inside her that made her feel brave, made her angry, made her right.

'Can you tell me where Finn is?'

'He's not taking visitors.' The nurse looked up as Ava strode over.

'He's taking this one!' Ava said, and she looked the nurse straight in the eye.

'Sorry, he's made it very clear…'

Ava turned to Hayley, who walked over, and asked again, but Hayley shook her head.

'Ava, he's not seeing anyone.'

'Go and tell him that Ava Carmichael is here and that if he refuses to see me then I'll tell everybody exactly what went on between us in the stairwell the night before his surgery.'

She stood there, cheeks flaming as she was the victim of yet more curious looks. The whole ward seemed to have stopped, even the domestic had stopped mopping, but actually Ava's cheeks were flaming in anger. She was past caring what the lot of them thought as she waited till Hayley returned.

'Has he said that he will see me?' Ava asked.

'Unfortunately, yes.' Hayley smiled. 'I was dying to find out what happened! Room four. Go on through.' Hayley caught Ava's arm as she walked past and then her voice was serious. 'Good luck.'

'Well, here she is!' Finn was at his most toxic—unshaven, the curtains drawn, he jeered as she walked into the room. 'The woman who left her husband in the middle of chemotherapy, her one-balled husband,' Finn added. 'The woman who had drunken sex in the stairwell…'

Ava just stood there as he insulted her, just knew, as Evie did, that it wasn't really Finn. 'That's what they'll all be saying now, you realise.'

'I don't care what they're saying.'

'Did we?' Finn asked. 'I've had so many drugs since admission, you know, I can't really remember that night.'

'Oh, you can remember,' Ava said. 'You can remember how scared you were and how badly you wanted Evie. You just don't want to remember, you just don't want to admit it. Well, here's a bit of advice, Finn—you can push people away, you can shut them out, you can deal with everything on your own, and then one day you might have to live with the consequences.' She faced him.

'I'm aware of the consequences, thank you.'

'Are you?' Ava asked. 'Are you quite sure about that? Because one day you might find out that Evie needs you, one day it might be her that's sitting on the oncology ward with a bag of poison going into her arm, and you've pushed so far, you've left it so long, that *he's* dealing with things on his own…'

'I thought you were here to see me…not talk about James.'

'I'm talking about you,' she shouted back—and she was.

Sort of.

'I'm talking about us both, but I'm *telling* you, one day something might happen and you might find yourself the one locked out of Evie's life—when, wheelchair or not, you could've been supporting her. Think about that as you wallow in your self-pity.'

'Get out!' he roared.

'I'm leaving already.'

She did. She had too much adrenaline and was far too angry to take the lift. She ran up the stairs and onto the oncology floor and, when he wasn't in his office, she found out where he was and spoke for several moments with a nurse, the one she'd seen him with in the canteen, in fact, before donning a gown and gloves and being allowed in.

James didn't look up.

He'd been dreading this morning, had made a grim joke to Harriet that he'd considered ringing in sick, and then she'd told him that Richard had, and in all honesty, James didn't blame him. And then he'd heard the nurses start talking.

'What's this about you and Finn on the stairwell?' He was flicking the remote for a DVD.

'Well, that didn't take long.' Ava rolled her eyes.

'Someone really ought to tell the nurses that that glass they stand behind isn't soundproof. Though don't,' James quickly added. 'I kind of like hearing what's going on.'

'Nothing happened between Finn and I except for a long conversation.'

'It's not my concern.'

'Maybe not,' Ava said. 'The same way I understand if you've been seeing someone…' She loved him so much that she spoke the truth. 'I know that I've been hell to live with. I promise you, I understand if there was someone else, but I'm not giving up on us without a fight.'

'Someone else? Er…' He gave her a very strange look. 'I'm not exactly living the single life at the moment.'

'I meant before,' Ava said, 'before we broke up.'

'I was never unfaithful.'

'Oh, please,' Ava said. 'I'm not stupid—we hadn't slept together in more than a year.'

'I know that,' James said, 'but there wasn't anybody else.'

'Don't lie about this, James,' she begged. 'We can't start again if we lie.'

'Ava, why would I sleep around when I'd been trying to save us?'

'So who were you ringing after your operation? I came back to talk and you were on the phone.' She could hear her jealousy, but she swallowed it down and misquoted him. '"Sorry about that, she's gone back to work now—we were nearly caught! Now where were we, Steph?"'

'I was trying to sort out the serviced apartment.' He had the audacity to laugh. 'Steph was very helpful, she's used to men planning on moving out and not telling their wives—though my situation was a touch more complicated. I wanted an end apartment, with the toilet furthest away from the adjoining wall…' She shook her head in impatience at his detail. 'Didn't want to upset the other guests.' He went back to his TV.

'So who were the linen trousers for? The posh new cologne? I mean it, James. I don't care… I mean, I understand if you…'

'They were for you.' He turned his head and

there was so much anger in his green eyes she almost believed him.

Almost, but she knew him too well and he knew her too well too.

'Liar,' she said. 'You know I don't care about things like that.'

'I told the marriage counsellor the same thing.' Ava couldn't believe what she was hearing.

'You went to a marriage counsellor?'

'When I was in Brisbane. Three months of it, telling her everything, and she still didn't get it—I mean, how do you explain us?'

'I don't know,' Ava admitted.

'Like I told her that you eat healthily and that you moaned about the way I ate and she said that maybe I'd let myself go a bit.'

'That wasn't what upset me,' Ava said. 'I just want you to take care of yourself.'

'Well, she said that maybe you wanted me to make more of an effort…'

'No!' She laughed. 'Well, you did look nice.'

'It was for you,' James said, and her heart seemed to squeeze in her chest. 'I joined a gym. I was out running every morning, bought new clothes, shaved, put on cologne, hell…' She could see the hurt and rejection right there on his face, and she winced at the recall of her reaction to him, or rather her complete lack of it. 'And I came home and you didn't give me a second glance.'

'I thought…' Oh, God, she really had thought it was for someone else. 'I thought you'd done it for someone else. And then I got the flowers. I thought you felt guilty, you never send me flowers.'

'Yeah, well, I did feel guilty. I was having a session with the counsellor when you rang, I got all flustered.' Guilty eyes looked up at her. 'I'd just told her we hadn't had sex in, like, for ever, and then you rang. It was as if you knew I was talking about us.'

'Oh, James.'

'She heard what I said, that I'd call you back, and she said that I handled the conversation all wrong, that I should send flowers. I said you didn't appreciate them. Still, it was worth a go…' She could not believe it, that James, her James, would sit and pour his heart out to a stranger, and she told him so. 'Two hundred dollars a week.' James was incredulous. 'The appointments had to be after hours, so it was two hundred dollars! What a damn waste.'

'It wasn't a waste.' She looked at him and could not believe all he had done to save them—how hard he had worked. And what had she done?

'Come home.' She saw him close his eyes. 'I want you home.'

'Ava.' He was so tired, too tired to fight and too tired to refuse, but also too tired to hurdle over this huge mound of pride. 'You don't have to feel sorry for me. I've only got a couple more rounds to go.'

'I don't want you back because I feel sorry for you. I want you back because I love you, because I can't stand us being apart. James, I do know how you feel.'

'No, Ava, you don't.'

'You think that I want to be there for all the wrong reasons. That if we get back together it will be because we have to rather than we want to? Well, guess what? I feel the same too.' She saw him frown. 'Watch this,' she said, handing him a DVD.

'Not more feel-good schmaltz,' James groaned. 'I don't need a single bit more inspiration…'

Ava said nothing as she put the DVD in. She watched his expression as he watched it.

'I'm fourteen weeks pregnant, James. Actually…' she did the maths '…I'm nearly fifteen.' And she watched him frown, watched him try to take it in. 'And in case you do ever wonder, nothing happened on the stairwell.'

'I know that,' James said, and he looked at his wife. 'Because I know you'd tell me if it did.'

'I would,' Ava said. 'And I don't have to because it didn't. We shared some whisky, spoke about Evie and I came inside and then I called you.'

He looked back at the screen, at their baby, and he rewound it and played it again.

'You should have told me.' She knew he wasn't talking about Finn. 'How could you not tell me?' Now he was angry. 'You didn't even try.'

And she opened her mouth to speak, to defend herself, to say that she had been to the serviced apartment to try, but she halted, because this was about them and nobody else needed to be included.

'How could I?' she asked, and it was up to him whether or not he would forgive her for keeping quiet. 'I might lose it,' Ava said. 'But I promise you this, if I do I will cry and I will sob, but I will grieve with you this time, and you will cry too, if you want to, and then I promise you that I will move on, because whatever happens I am so grateful because this baby make me see sense…'

He still wouldn't give in, so she told him the truth. Was as direct with James as she'd been with Finn. 'That's your daughter or son there, and if this pregnancy does last…' They'd let things go so far, she just didn't know if they could claw back from it—but they had to.

'Do you just want access visits, James? Alternate weekends?' And it must have hit him somewhere inside, because he put his hand up to stop her, but she continued. 'I'll have Christmas mornings, please, and then you can take it to your mum's for lunch, or to your girlfriend's, or whatever…'

'Stop it.'

‘No!’ She would not stop. ‘Because that’s how it will be.’

‘No.’ And she watched her proud, strong man start crying, and it was the first time she had ever seen him cry, not held-back tears, not angry tears, just tears, and he was too tired to even wipe them away. He just sat in the chair so, so defeated, and she could see him bald and thin and yet still so proud and just perhaps the most honest and beautiful she had ever seen James, and she couldn’t simply hold him and kiss away his tears, so instead she stood in gown and gloves and she stayed strong.

‘Or you can come back to me today and I’ll never really know if you’re just coming back for the baby. I’ve got the golden ticket, haven’t I?’

And she thought the same as he did, James realised, felt the same as he did, was simply a part of him. ‘I’ve got the reason for you to come back…’

'Ava, all I want is to be with you, baby or no baby, that's all I ever wanted.' And she was scared to believe him too.

'Should you be here?' She smiled when he said it, when he looked up at the drip, because he was as terrified as her. 'I mean, with the chemo…'

'I spoke to the nurse when I came in. I have to be careful with your body fluids for the next forty-eight hours, but I'm upping it to seventy-two hours…' She gave him a little wink, but she was terrified of that part too—of chemo and the effects on the baby—but she couldn't live like that any longer, couldn't kill her marriage again.

'I've had whisky, though of course I didn't know I was pregnant then and Marco said not to worry, I probably needed a bit of sedation that night. And I'm swimming…' she looked at him '…and riding.'

'Before you found out?' James said, because he knew how she was.

'No.' She shook her head. 'Yesterday I went horse riding and I went riding the day before too and for the first time since you found that lump, for a couple of hours I felt great, and the baby is still here and holding on…'

'Are we?'

'Yes,' she said. 'Yes.' She said it again and she was crying now too, and because she couldn't kiss him, instead she took that weary face she loved so much into her gloved hands. She hadn't touched his face in so long—it was relief, sheer relief to hold him, and the relief was mixed with frustration because she could only wipe away his tears through the rubber gloves.

And Ava, once practical, the moment she held him again believed, in kindred spirits and angels and a love that was meant to be. And James, who thought you just died and were buried, believed just a little too as he held her again, because it felt like nothing he could explain.

Not stir-fried rice and chicken and unconditional love, but this danger that came with the woman in his arms. And yet there was a sense of safety too.

She knew him.

She was the only person he wanted to be with and he didn't want to do this alone any more.

'I know you won't believe me,' James said, 'I know you think I'm just saying it, but that morning before I found it, I was thinking about you, I wanted you to come into the shower with me but I thought that might be pushing it so I was going to come out and talk. I wanted us to maybe try again.'

'James.' She didn't care about the nurses behind the glass partition. Let them hear, she thought, let them see, because she loved him so much she was fine if the whole world knew it. 'What did you think I was coming into the shower for?' She saw him frown and she started to laugh, because the truth was so obvious now. 'I could hear you, you big idiot. You're not exactly quiet when you get it on!'

She saw him smile, she could hear her baby's heartbeat on the screen as the two of them remembered the night that it was made, and she told him her truth, a truth that had been lost in the pain of these past weeks.

'What do you think I was coming into the bathroom for, James? I was coming in to be with you.'

CHAPTER FIFTEEN

AND they tumbled into bed.

Except it didn't happen.

She wanted that.

Knew he did too.

Except it was more private than that for both of them. More difficult than, even in her job capacity, she had ever understood.

He puked his way through the first three days after chemo and she tried not to hover at the door, and he shouted to her once not to come in when she went to, because he didn't want her holding his head, but he did love the endless flannels she soaked in ice, and he conceded and drank her protein shakes when he could keep things down and ate Brazil nuts because Ava believed they would help.

She cooked for two.

Different sorts of meals from before, but this time they ate the same—because she'd been trawling the internet and was obsessed with his diet now instead of hers. And she got now how Veronica had needed to cook, needed to feed him, needed to do something, and she smiled and chatted much more graciously when Veronica came round. They had a baby to talk about so that made things easier too. Then, one evening James was called in for a patient. 'Richard,' he told Ava, because he told her more about his work now. Richard had come back for his treatment yesterday but had been admitted because he was febrile and James, of course, was straight out of the door. Instead of scuttling off, Veronica actually hung around and they chatted awkwardly for a moment and then Ava made tea.

'That time you came around…' Ava's hand was shaking as she pulled out the teabag as

Veronica asked the question… 'Did you know you were pregnant then?'

'I'd just found out,' Ava said.

'You'd come to tell him?' Veronica swallowed as Ava nodded. 'James would never forgive me if he found out.'

'And he never will find out,' Ava said. 'And you're wrong, James would forgive you.'

'Can you?'

'I did ages ago,' Ava said, because she'd done an awful lot of thinking—about how hard it must be for Veronica at times to be the one left to carry on. 'It didn't feel like it at the time, but being apart…' She closed her eyes for a moment because it was so hard to explain it and she never wanted to be apart from him again, but just as she had said to George and Elise, from something so awful good things had come. She'd been with James since she was eighteen, had only ever been with James, and had relied on his love perhaps a little too much.

Now she knew that if she had to she could make it on her own and so could James. And in their uncertain worlds it brought them both comfort, and Ava knew also that she would never take his love for granted again. 'We're stronger for it.'

And the two women just tried harder, because they had one thing in common at least—they both loved James.

And he loved Ava, so he let her add the blueberries to his oat bran and he cut down on carbs, but he still insisted on sugar in his coffee, and at night they cuddled sometimes and other times slept on their own sides of the bed, and for the next couple of weeks they sort of learned how to share their lives again.

Just not that part.

Oh, they were sharing a bed now and sometimes she woke up in his arms, but they just hadn't got to where they fell asleep like that. She lay in bed this morning and all she wanted was a kiss. They'd had a couple, but sort of awkward ones, and she stared up at the dark and went through her faults.

Yes, she was practical at work but completely neurotic at home, and then she thought some more, went over their rows before they'd got back together, went over the one where he'd admitted that he was scared, and she grimaced as she recalled his words.

I'm patronising. She groaned in her head.

I am—she reluctantly concluded—*he was completely right. If they had been together when he'd been diagnosed she'd have been terribly efficient about sex and so, so annoyingly understanding.*

She actually made herself laugh as she thought about it, just lay in the dark and let out a giggle because, yes, at times she could be a right royal pain.

Maybe she should get up and have a shower.

Except she'd run out of conditioner *again*,

but she'd bought some last week, she was quite sure of it.

'Don't look at me,' James said when she'd accused him last night of pinching her expensive stuff. 'What would I need conditioner for?'

She was disorganised too, Ava decided.

And then she felt something—something she'd been chasing, something that it felt like she'd been waiting for for ever, and it came the moment it wasn't on her mind.

This flutter in her stomach.

So fleeting, so vague, and of course it must be wind.

Except she felt it again.

Like a tiny mouse scratching from the inside.

'It moved.'

Her fifth pregnancy and she'd never felt her baby move, and she was now completely certain that it was.

'What?' Already woken by her mad, morning laughter James rolled over to face her on his side.

'The baby…'

He put her hand to her stomach and of course he couldn't feel the little mouse scratching.

'I felt it.'

'I know,' James said, because, well, Ava didn't say things that hadn't happened—she was far too practical with her body for that. So he held his hand on her tummy for a full sixty seconds and, no, he couldn't feel it, and got a bit bored maybe waiting, because all by itself his hand wandered…

It just did.

Over a body that was changing, and his hand traced her stomach and then dusted down—it said hello to her thighs, but didn't greet her knees before it worked its way back up.

She felt each stroke and then she felt his caution, the wait for her to say no, or for her to say she was tired, or needed space, or a panicked reminder about the *baby*! But instead she felt his mouth on her breast and, God, she loved his mouth, and she let her thighs relax and felt his fingers explore, and as controlling as she was, it was his fingers that controlled her then.

'Ava…'

He slipped his fingers in where she lay, loose-legged, and the very solid nudge of him every now and then told her that he was just as fine as she was. She lay there and didn't think about saline balls, or chemo, or that he was bald, or that she had a baby on board and a womb that could collapse at a moment's notice. She just thought about the lovely things he was doing to her and the lovely things she was doing to him too.

And she listened to their noise.

And James was usually noisy, but this morning it was she, moaning and groaning and giving Kirribilli Views their wake-up call of old.

'I'm going to come.' She said it in panic, because she should surely be the calm, reassuring one, insisting on taking things nice and slowly, except she couldn't.

'Come,' he said as his fingers brought her closer. 'I want to watch.'

And her books went out of the window; she should be so much more laid back, so much more...*thoughtful.*

Except she wanted him. Was she terrible that that was all she wanted?

'Come inside me!'

He was inside her in a minute.

He moved over her, split her apart with his thighs and there he was on top, her hands grabbing at shoulders, thinner than she remembered at uni but so much stronger their union now, and this was their glorious moment, because eyes never changed.

Green eyes gazed at her.

Loving her as together they came.

James.

Ava.

Worth fighting for.

EPILOGUE

'YOU'D turned them off.'

James gave a wry smile as he walked into the room.

Right at the end of her labour, when things had suddenly become tense, Ava had remembered that she might have left her hair straighteners on. Actually, she was quite sure she had, because she'd been straightening her hair for her antenatal appointment when all the drama had started, trying to tell herself that the contractions she was having were nothing to get excited about, they were probably Braxton-Hicks. Marco had warned her that her baby was a big one, and was today going to talk about inducing her, or even recommend she consider a Caesarean, which Ava definitely didn't want. Except that as she'd stood there pondering how soon he might induce her, and just how much bigger she could possibly get, her waters had broken and things had moved surprisingly quickly from then on.

'James?'

He'd heard her voice from the bathroom and even before he'd walked in there he'd known.

And he'd known how terrified she was too.

And he had been terrified as well, but not for a moment had he shown it, especially when by ten minutes later she was already two heavy contractions in, and four heavy contractions in by the time he'd been put through to Maternity to tell them they were on their way.

'Ring your mum!' Ava had ordered as they'd headed for the door, because Veronica had asked to be kept up to date with all news.

'She'll want to come,' James had said as she'd doubled up at the door. 'We'll ring her afterwards.'

'By the time she gets there,' Ava gritted, 'it will be afterwards.'

She was almost right.

There was something about Finn and lifts because as they stepped inside he was on his way down, dressed in a suit and on his way to work, his last day at work before his operation next week.

And after a brief good morning he suitably ignored them, because there were certain times you didn't want to be seen—except the lift wasn't moving and it was James rather frantically pushing the buttons and then there was nothing prim about Ava, Finn noted as she cursed like a navvy and pressed the buttons herself, because she was not going down by the stairwell and she was not having her baby here. But thankfully the lift started moving and as Finn got out at the ground floor while they headed down for the car in the basement, he had the decency to simply step out.

Emily, who was quite pregnant herself, examined her on arrival.

'We might just see about getting the doctor down.' She'd given Ava the nicest smile and had called out to a colleague and then quietly set up for delivery as Ava bore down.

'It's too fast…' Ava begged, because her mind couldn't catch up with the speed of things, and it was then she remembered the hair straighteners and that she might have left them on.

Marco, when she said it again, had told her to forget such things.

'Ava, don't worry about that now.' He said it very calmly. In fact, had she not been his wife, Emily might not have noted the slight tension in his voice, and she looked down to where the head that was almost out, and then it retracted. It was called 'turtle sign' and indicative of shoulder dystocia. Emily noted that James was a big guy, with very broad shoulders, and she saw James watching too, saw the dart of nervousness in his eyes, and Emily took a calming breath as Ava ranted about the hair straighteners, and her patient did not need to know what was happening yet, she was terrified enough.

'Nice slow breath, Ava,' Emily said. 'Let that thought go. Your baby's nearly here and then James can go home and check on those straighteners for you. Now, let's bring your legs right up.' She took one leg and James the other to open up the pelvis some more, and James told her that, yes, soon he'd go home, that she could stop worrying about that now.

And that helped her to stop terrifying herself, convincing herself, in fact, that as she laboured on, the flat was burning down, which meant the contracts wouldn't go through on the house they had bought.

Yes, they had a house.

The one she'd imagined James walking into, with kids hanging off him and clearly at peace with his saline ball, except she hadn't been walking past with frozen meals and vegetables and cat food. Instead, she had been sitting on the veranda, watching her family be.

And it was the house of her dreams. She simply hadn't recognised it then. It was the house where they had first made love. It had come onto the market three weeks after they'd got back together and everyone had said they were crazy, that they had far too much on their plates without buying an old bomb.

Except they'd fallen in love with it.

And Ava had co-ordinated the renovators and now, if not quite finished, they were ready to move in and the contracts for the flat were going through this week.

It would be there that they brought home their baby.

'You're doing great, Ava,' James said, his voice strong and calm, even though fear ripped through him at the potential precariousness of the situation as he watched his baby struggle to be born. Just for a second he wondered why things had to be so hard for them, wondered just how much more they could take, and then almost instantly he shoved that thought aside because life, too, had been wonderful to them and they could take whatever it sent them.

'Just relax a moment before the next one, Ava.' And she did as he said and relaxed just a little, just breathed for a moment, and the rest of the room breathed too as her pelvis opened that necessary fraction more, and then in a moment her new family was there, her baby being lifted onto her stomach, and there was this breeze of joy and relief and love that swept into the room.

James cut the cord and shook hands with Marco and nothing was said—because today she really didn't need to know, but, yes, if there were to be any more baby Carmichaels then it would be a Caesarean next time.

No, today Ava didn't need to know what a close call it had been for a moment.

Today she just had to concentrate on being a mum.

And so, after they'd cuddled their son and just marvelled at him, they had opened the door to Veronica, and there had been cuddles and kisses all around. Ava thought it was nice to have her there, nice to share the joy, nice to be happy but a little bit wistful too.

'I wish your dad was here.'

'So do I,' James admitted, and again Ava understood Veronica a bit more.

'What did your parents say?' Veronica asked. 'They must be beside themselves.

'They will be when they pick up their voicemail,' Ava said, understanding her own parents a little less, and she felt James's hand squeeze her shoulder just a bit tighter. And just as she was being moved to her room, James had felt her tense and in the end had given her a kiss and popped home to check that she had turned the straighteners off.

And, yes, just as they hadn't at the start of their relationship, no longer did those sorts of things annoy him.

Well, maybe very occasionally, but they knew what was important now.

'I'm going to buy you the sort that turn off themselves,' Veronica offered when James came back and gave the inevitable all-clear.

'Well, can you buy her an iron that turns itself off as well, then,' James said. 'Oh, and an oven that turns itself off when you close the front door...' He looked at their new surroundings. 'Nice room.'

It was a wonderful room, with an amazing view—a view that so often had soothed her, a view that was there patiently waiting to see her through good times and bad, and she was infinitely grateful for it.

'Here!'

He handed her flowers.

Pale flowers with hardly a trace of scent. Iceberg roses from the bushes she had planted in their new garden.

Her very favourite kind.

'Teo's just giving him the once-over,' Ava said, as the paediatrician turned and gave James a smile.

'He's perfect.' Teo finished examining him and handed Baby Carmichel to James. 'Welcome to the sleepless-nights club,' he said.

'Yep,' James shook his hand while with the other he held his son. 'I hear you're a recent member.'

'Zoe came home yesterday.'

And when Teo had gone and the lunches were being brought out, Veronica did the most amazing thing.

'Well, I'm going to head home.' Ava nearly fell off the bed.

'Stay!' she offered, and peered at a very unappetising beef stroganoff. 'James can go out and get something nice for lunch…'

'That rabbit food you two eat?' Veronica frowned. 'No, thanks.' But then she did give Ava a smile because, after all, James was doing very well on it—even if Ava was convinced he was cheating an awful lot of the time. 'Anyway, I've got a lot of phone calls to make. I'll come in this evening, though—if that's okay?'

'That'd be great.'

'Do you need anything? Anything you want me to bring in?'

'Some of your chicken and fried rice maybe?' Ava said, because they'd cheat together tonight. 'And champagne.' She grinned.

'Already in the fridge,' Veronica said, and gave her grandson just one more cuddle before she was gone.

Not that they were alone for long.

Word had got out and the gift shop must be

running hot because the domestic kept ferrying in balloons and bunches of flowers

'We take them out at night,' she assured them.

Well, they weren't taking out her iceberg roses, Ava decided.

And James read the cards out to her as she fed their son.

George was in to see Donald and we heard the news!
So happy for you both.
George and Elise
(Playing lots of Scrabble) xxx

'Who are George and Elise and why are they playing lots of Scrabble?' James frowned and then stopped frowning as he got it, because sometimes now she did bring her work home with her, even if he didn't know it, and they were playing lots of Scrabble too—and walking on the beach and, yes, lots of talking and, yes, things would remain fine.

They'd both see to it.

'Oh, and I texted Richard with the news...' James said, because, given all they had been through, Richard had become far more than a patient, 'He rang straight back, he's thrilled, and,' James added, 'he's got some news of his own. We've got an engagement party to go to in a few weeks.'

And then he went to read out another one but he just stopped and laughed.

'Who's it from?' Ava asked.

'Guess.' James grinned.

Welcome to Baby Carmichael
Remembering the stairwell fondly,
Finn (Actually it's Evie, he'd never think to send flowers) xxx

'Well, that's going to silence the rumour mill.' James laughed and then it faded, because the gift shop was going to be extra-busy in the next few days too. 'I hope his surgery goes well for him.'

'It will,' Ava said.

'You don't know that,' James said, because now he did stress a little, well, he always had, as it turned out, he'd just not told her.

And now he did.

'It's a big gamble,' James said. 'All or nothing this time…'

'Well, whatever the outcome, Finn will deal with it,' Ava said. 'And we'll all be there for him—whether the grumpy old goat wants it or not.'

And she looked down at her son, whose eyes seemed to reach into her heart.

'He's huge.' He had a squashed-up face like a boxer's and was sucking hungrily on his fist despite having been fed twice, and somehow he reminded her so much of his dad that it made her laugh.

'If there is a next time, I'm having a Caesarean.' She caught his eyes and he knew that she knew, but sometimes you didn't need to go over things.

'Yes, Ava,' James said. 'You are.'

And then she looked back at her baby and couldn't quite believe he was here. She peeled off the little beanie that was on his head and tufted the pale brown hair. 'He's got more hair than you.'

'Not for long,' James said, because it was growing back, and he looked at his wife and climbed up on the bed beside her.

'He looks like an Eddie,' Ava said, and James looked at his son who looked like him, and he thought of his own dad and he smiled.

'Text your mum his name,' Ava said, 'so she can tell everyone.'

And James did, texted a photo of his son to his mother, so she could forward the image of

Edward James Carmichael to the people she couldn't wait to tell.

And then the Emily stopped by on her way home and told her how well she had done.

'Thanks so much,' Ava said. 'And Marco too—you were both great.'

'I'm on in the morning.' Emily smiled. 'I'll come in and we can go through your labour,' she said, because by tomorrow or maybe the next day Ava would want to, but for now she needed to rest, just as her son was.

'Do you want me to put him in his crib?' Emily offered, and when Ava nodded she took a not so little Eddie and popped him in his crib and then suggested she could close the curtains and turn the lights down and, given the traffic from the gift shop, maybe a 'no visitors' sign on the door.

'Please,' Ava said, because she loved them all and everything, but there would be time for that tonight, time to share their good news with everyone. She just wanted to be with her husband now and, yes, the view was to die for, but it would still be there when she needed it. She needed some time with James more.

He was clean-shaven, wearing those grey linen trousers and he smelt just a little of cologne as he pulled her into him, and it was all for her.

'Fancy a second honeymoon?' James said. 'Just us three?'

'Yes, please.'

'Beach?'

Ava closed her eyes and shook her head.

'Mountains?' She shook her head again.

'Home,' she said. 'Let's honeymoon at home.' And she thought of their house and their garden that was waiting and the man who lay beside her and just how far the two of them had come, how much deeper their love now was, and she simply couldn't be happier.

'Let's enjoy every precious day.'

* * * * *

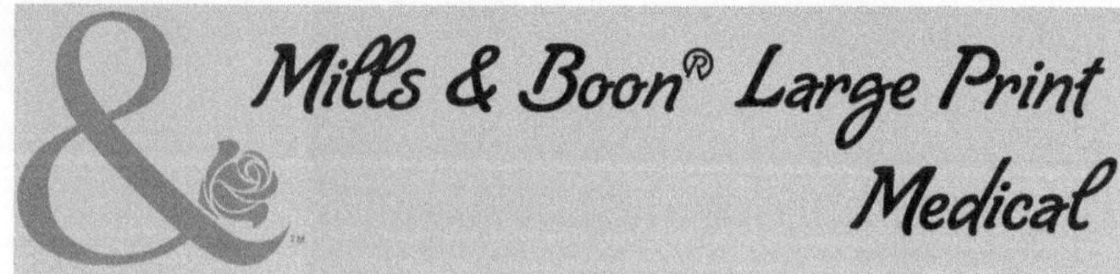

March

HER MOTHERHOOD WISH	Anne Fraser
A BOND BETWEEN STRANGERS	Scarlet Wilson
ONCE A PLAYBOY...	Kate Hardy
CHALLENGING THE NURSE'S RULES	Janice Lynn
THE SHEIKH AND THE SURROGATE MUM	Meredith Webber
TAMED BY HER BROODING BOSS	Joanna Neil

April

A SOCIALITE'S CHRISTMAS WISH	Lucy Clark
REDEEMING DR RICCARDI	Leah Martyn
THE FAMILY WHO MADE HIM WHOLE	Jennifer Taylor
THE DOCTOR MEETS HER MATCH	Annie Claydon
THE DOCTOR'S LOST-AND-FOUND HEART	Dianne Drake
THE MAN WHO WOULDN'T MARRY	Tina Beckett

May

MAYBE THIS CHRISTMAS...?	Alison Roberts
A DOCTOR, A FLING & A WEDDING RING	Fiona McArthur
DR CHANDLER'S SLEEPING BEAUTY	Melanie Milburne
HER CHRISTMAS EVE DIAMOND	Scarlet Wilson
NEWBORN BABY FOR CHRISTMAS	Fiona Lowe
THE WAR HERO'S LOCKED-AWAY HEART	Louisa George

June

FROM CHRISTMAS TO ETERNITY	Caroline Anderson
HER LITTLE SPANISH SECRET	Laura Iding
CHRISTMAS WITH DR DELICIOUS	Sue MacKay
ONE NIGHT THAT CHANGED EVERYTHING	Tina Beckett
CHRISTMAS WHERE SHE BELONGS	Meredith Webber
HIS BRIDE IN PARADISE	Joanna Neil

July

THE SURGEON'S DOORSTEP BABY	Marion Lennox
DARE SHE DREAM OF FOREVER?	Lucy Clark
CRAVING HER SOLDIER'S TOUCH	Wendy S. Marcus
SECRETS OF A SHY SOCIALITE	Wendy S. Marcus
BREAKING THE PLAYBOY'S RULES	Emily Forbes
HOT-SHOT DOC COMES TO TOWN	Susan Carlisle

August

THE BROODING DOC'S REDEMPTION	Kate Hardy
AN INESCAPABLE TEMPTATION	Scarlet Wilson
REVEALING THE REAL DR ROBINSON	Dianne Drake
THE REBEL AND MISS JONES	Annie Claydon
THE SON THAT CHANGED HIS LIFE	Jennifer Taylor
SWALLOWBROOK'S WEDDING OF THE YEAR	Abigail Gordon

0213 LP 2P P2 Medical